Out
≥ of the ≤
Clouds

Out
of the
Clouds

Diana Hendry

Hodder
Children's
Books

First published in Great Britain in 2016 by Hodder Children's Books
This edition published in 2018 by Hodder Children's Books

The poem Ma reads on page 111 is from 'A Red, Red Rose' by Robert Burns.
The 'jolly song' Olly hears his pa singing on page 173 is from Gilbert and
Sullivan's opera, H.M.S. *Pinafore*.

1 3 5 7 9 10 8 6 4 2

A Catalogue record for this book is available from the British Library

ISBN 978 1 444 92477 0

Hodder Children's Books
A division of Hachette Children's Group
Part of Hodder & Stoughton
Carmelite House,
50 Victoria Embankment,
London, EC4Y 0DZ

An Hachette UK Company
www.hachette.co.uk

For Ruairidh
with love from Granny

To begin . . .

In the village of Starwater the locals never tired of talking about the strange, sea-battered house that looked down on them from high up on the cliffs. The tall, narrow house, with its wonky windows, half-hinged shutters, ridiculous balconies and a tower like a Christmas cracker hat plonked on top, was known as *Dizzy Perch*.

You had the feeling that whoever had built it would have liked to go on and on adding floor after floor, as if he or she had a skyscraper in mind. But who had built it? And why?

Someone who'd wanted to get away from the world perhaps?

Someone who'd run away and was hiding?

A poet with a big big poem to write?

A musician – a drummer or trombonist – who made a lot of noise?

A mad person's folly? But why was *Dizzy Perch* so big if it was just for one person?

Almost as strange as the house was the family who had come to live there.

If you happened to linger outside Starwater's Post Office Stores, or stand waiting at the bus stop, or walk past the twelve cottages of Seaview Terrace, or wander along the harbour wall, you couldn't help but hear all the questions that flew about the village; much as the seagulls did when the fishing boats came in with a catch.

Sometimes it would be the women standing in a huddle outside the stores:

'*Who'd want to live up there?*'

'*They must be hiding something . . .*'

'*Or in trouble . . .*'

'*Or up to no good.*'

'*Three children . . .*

'*Up in a place no one can get to . . .*'

'*And you never saw her.*'

2

'*Is there a* him?'

And then there'd be a lot of shaking of heads.

Sometimes it would be a couple of old men leaning on the harbour wall.

'*'Course it has a history, that house.*'

'*Doubt it's a good one.*'

'*Some say it's haunted . . .*'

'*Well, there are tales . . .*'

'*Have you heard the fiddle?*'

'*Late at night, when it's very quiet. Wife says it's the old man.*'

Or you might hear Mrs Dubbins of 2 Seaview Terrace as she pegs the washing out and has a morning gossip with her neighbour, Mrs Loxley.

'*I seen the boy. The clothes that child wears!*'

'*Mine wouldn't be seen dead . . .*'

'*And the old man?*'

'*Looks like a tramp?*'

'*Where have they come from?*'

'*And what are they up to?*'

'*Does anyone know their name?*'

And on they go, tongues and washing

flapping happily.

If you should happen to go into the Post Office Stores and ask Mrs Emma Tansley, who runs the Stores *and* the Post Office (the two being quite a trouble to her) about the family who have come to live in *Dizzy Perch*, she could tell you their name.

'Coggin,' she'd say. 'Coggin's their name. The elder boy is called Oliver Coggin.' And that's all she'd be likely to tell you because Mrs Tansley had become quite fond of Oliver Coggin and sorry for him too, turning up in those strange clothes his mother (or someone) dresses him in and having to do all the shopping and carry it up the cliff. And sorry too because she knew Oliver hears the villagers talking about him and his family and she could see from the way his face flushes and his eyes look a bit watery and his gingery hair stands on end, that it upsets him.

Not that Mrs Tansley wasn't curious. She was. But not in an unkind way. And mostly she was sorriest of all that whenever Oliver asked her, which he always did, *Any letters for Coggin?* she had to duck under the Stores counter, come up the other side to the Post Office Counter, put on her postmistress hat and, after all that, say, 'Sorry dear, not today,' and watch him trying to hide his disappointment.

And though she didn't ask, she couldn't help but wonder – who was Oliver Coggin expecting a letter from?

CHAPTER 1

The Coggins of Dizzy Perch

Oliver Coggin was sad. He was sad in the way someone is sad when there's no one to share their sadness with. Sad in the way sadness grows and hangs on your heart like a heavy weight. Sad in the way sadness gets mixed up with all sorts of other things like crossness and grumpiness and feeling sorry for yourself.

It was not the morning for feeling sad. It was a bright spring morning and *Dizzy Perch* was full of sunshine. Sunshine shone the kitchen pans, played light-and-shadow on the walls, shivered the sea far, far down below with silver crests. Sometimes Oliver thought there was something not unlike a lighthouse about *Dizzy*

Perch. Whichever window you looked from, all you could see was sea.

Sunshine didn't help Oliver's sadness. Breakfast was over and, as usual, Oliver had been left with the dishes. And as usual, everyone else – that is, Ma, Lottie, Titch and Grandpa – had munched and jollied their way through porridge, toast, bananas (Titch) and tea without one of them even mentioning the gap at the breakfast table, the gap in the Coggin family. Pa. Off they'd all fled – as if they were afraid that sadness, like a cold, might be catching – each to their own obsession: Ma to her books, Lottie to her dressing-up trunk in the tower, Titch to his pebble collection, Grandpa to his fiddle or his workshop.

'Dear Thing!' Ma said, as she said every morning (for all her children were 'Dear Things'), patting Oliver's shoulder as she left the kitchen, licking a little marmalade off her fingers.

Oliver gathered up the plates and bowls and dumped them in the sink.

When he'd finished the dishes, Oliver went to the calendar that hung on the back door and crossed off another day. Another day without Pa. It was March twenty-first. How long was it now since he'd settled them all in *Dizzy Perch*? He'd mended the leaks in the roof, attended to a broken shutter, made a wonderful funicular railway so that they could get up and down the cliff, and had gone off, swinging a large rucksack on his back. He'd hugged Oliver as if he'd wanted to print his shadow on Oliver's heart, and waved to them all as if he was just going down to the village and back. Only he wasn't and he didn't.

That had been in the autumn. Oliver had hoped – surely they'd *all* hoped – he'd be back for Christmas. Oliver had heard Grandpa shouting at Ma, as if it was Ma's fault – 'What kind of a father is it who doesn't come home for Christmas?' And Ma's almost apologetic answer – 'You know how it is. He would if he could.' To which Grandpa had snorted, '*Hrumph!*'

To Oliver, Lottie and Titch, Ma said, 'Pa has

very important work to do. Secret work that keeps him away.'

'Which is why we're up here, out of harm's way,' said Grandpa. But Ma had frowned at him, as if Grandpa had said something he shouldn't.

Oliver often pondered Grandpa's comment. It was true that *Dizzy Perch* was out of the way of most things. Things that Oliver rather hankered after, like shops, friends and neighbours. A garden. Even a school! But 'harm'? Did wildness not count as harm? The house was surrounded by it – swirling mists, whirling gulls, fierce winds, stormy seas lashing the cliffs. Wind made the house rock and groan, rain (despite Pa's mendings) had to be caught in buckets. When it snowed, as it had done in November, Grandpa had had to make them sledges because the funicular railway seized up. Oliver often had the feeling that *Dizzy Perch* was just clinging on, that with a really bad storm it could be ripped from its roots.

And there was something else. Somehow it was impossible to live here – *nesting* was what it felt like, nesting like the seagulls and gannets, or the rooks that cawed and crackled as if they knew exactly what 'harm' meant – without the wildness getting inside you. As if all of them, all the Coggins, landed here, as Oliver thought of it, with only themselves for company, were slowly turning as wild as the birds.

It was partly to keep the wildness at bay that Oliver had taken on the cooking and cleaning and tidying of *Dizzy Perch*. And partly because as far as he could tell, the others seemed to think that meals appeared, rooms were tidied, bathrooms were cleaned, magically, overnight, maybe by a team of elves otherwise known as Oliver. *Oliver likes doing it*, was what they thought, if they thought anything at all. *So we'll let him do it.* And in a way this was true. Oliver liked the way you could mix things together in a bowl, put the mix in a tin in the oven and, *Hey presto!* half an hour later, out came a cake. *Ta ra!* And he liked wandering about the house. Sometimes he thought that Ma, Titch, Lottie and Grandpa were so wrapped up in their own doings that unless he called in on them – with the pretext of tidying – none of them would bother talking to him. Or each other. And sometimes he just liked wandering about the house listening to – well, the house itself.

Once he'd put the kitchen in order, Oliver put a big yellow bag over his shoulder (for collecting up lost items). He put a notebook and pencil in his pocket for Ma's morning instructions and carried a bucket with a brush and shovel and a wet cloth for any messes he might find.

The Coggins were glad *Dizzy Perch* was large. It meant they each had a room. The kitchen spread across two rooms on the ground floor and opened on to the rocks at the back. The sitting room was on the first floor and next to it Pa's study. A very narrow hall ran across the width of the house with the front door in the middle. From there, great stone steps led down to the funicular railway.

On the floor above Ma and Grandpa each had a room with a covered balcony tacked on at the front. Were they there as look-outs? Or for bird-watching? Sunbathing? Storm-viewing? Grandpa had a telescope on his. Ma had a big comfy wicker chair with a quantity of cushions on hers. There was a cranky bathroom and lavatory between the two rooms.

Titch and Oliver had the next floor (with another cranky bathroom and lavatory between) and Lottie, who had been growing her hair ever since they'd moved in so she could be Rapunzel, had the tower which was made of clapboard and looked as if it had been an afterthought. It had one small window and a slit as if for arrows. Attached to the side of the house, and reached by the back door, was a long shed roofed in slates that blew off in the wind and which Grandpa had commandeered as his workshop.

The sitting room was the comfiest room in the house. Several old sofas with sunken seats and battered arms had come to rest there as had a few cushions Ma no longer had any room for. There was a faded rug that still held some of its former brightness, a bookshelf and a wood-burning stove that Grandpa supplied with logs and which Oliver kept going in winter. There was always lost property – Oliver picked up a chisel (Grandpa's), two books (Ma's), a velvet cloak (Lottie's), and a tin full of coloured sea-glass (Titch's) and put them all in his yellow bag.

He looked in at Pa's study next. There was no point in looking, really. It remained perfectly tidy. There was a dry, dusty smell about it, about the desk and the chest that was kept locked and the table with its line-up of empty test-tubes and measuring funnels. Without Pa it was as if the room had died. Did rooms need people, Oliver wondered, to keep them alive? And was he the only one who missed Pa? Had they all forgotten him? Even Ma? Even Grandpa? Did no one talk about him because they didn't care about him? Were they even glad Pa wasn't around? It was true Pa could be very bossy and that he had a quick temper. But it *was* quick. Over and done with and then he made it up to you. Oliver stood there with his eyes closed trying to conjure up Pa. It was no good. With a sigh he closed the door, and went up the spiral staircase. He never bothered taking the rope ladder up to Lottie's tower. It was a mass of materials and clothes, costumes, paints and papers. There was no point in even attempting to tidy it or Lottie. Oliver could hear her singing to herself and knew that she had her window open and was making something that she would probably be wearing later in the day.

Oliver swept up a trail of wood shavings that had spread, like confetti, down the spiral staircase and along the hall from Grandpa's room. Sometimes Oliver thought that Grandpa was like a wet dog that shook itself and showered everyone with water. Unless Oliver reminded him, Grandpa mostly forgot to change his clothes. He simply shook himself free of wood shavings. You could follow Grandpa wherever he went by the wood shavings. Grandpa's room was Oliver's favourite. Apart from anything else, Grandpa had his own kettle, as well as a small camping stove (that Ma said was a fire hazard), as well as a tin of drinking chocolate and another of biscuits. Oliver reasoned it was that time of the morning when both would be welcome.

Oliver was just about to knock on the door – a courtesy Grandpa insisted on – when to his surprise he heard voices, Grandpa's and Ma's, both of them in Ma's room. At least out on Ma's balcony. Oliver didn't have to eavesdrop, their voices carried. Grandpa's cross. Ma's soothing.

'But how d'you know?' Grandpa was asking. 'How d'you know he's not in trouble?'

'He'd have sent word,' said Ma. 'You know he warned us this might take a long time.'

'Not this long,' said Grandpa. 'And sending word has never been something that son of mine has been much good at. If you'd just let me have the key to the chest, then at least we might know *where* he is, even if we don't know *how* he is.'

'He doesn't want us to know where he is,' said Ma. 'That's the whole point. If we don't know where he is, we can't tell anyone.'

'But who's there to tell?' Grandpa's voice seemed to have gone up an octave.

'Look,' said Ma. 'All I know is that I promised. Promised not to open the chest unless there was an emergency.'

'And you'll know when that is, will you?' demanded Grandpa.

'Yes,' said Ma.

'He's always been doing experiments,' said Grandpa. 'And none of them have been hush-hush like this. None of them have been dangerous. None of them have kept him away for ages. And anyway, if he's been kidnapped and gagged in a cell somewhere, sending word won't be very easy, will it?'

'Well, now you're letting your imagination run away with you,' said Ma in what Oliver recognised as her most reasonable and comforting voice. (Oliver's own imagination was already running alongside Grandpa's. He knelt near the door feeling suddenly cold and shivery like the beginning of flu.) 'I think you're just feeling your age. Getting anxious when

17

there's no need,' Ma continued.

'Of course I'm getting anxious,' shouted Grandpa. 'And it's got nothing to do with age, my girl. It's to do with responsibility. It's to do with being a father before being whatever else he is.'

'A scientist?' ventured Ma. 'An inventor?'

'Fiddlesticks!' cried Grandpa. 'Why can't he do all that here? Why can't he be here with you, with his children?'

There was a creaking of chairs, a slam of the balcony door. Oliver hurried back down the staircase. Grandpa was at the door. Oliver heard Ma call after him: 'Whatever he's doing, it's important for the future. He told me that himself.'

'The future!' growled Grandpa. 'I've not much of that left.'

Oliver slid down the last steps of the staircase and busied himself in the kitchen. Grandpa slammed out of the back on the way to his workshop.

Oliver hung the big yellow bag on the peg

18

and put away the bucket. There were just too many questions in his head. Important, secret work – well, that was worry enough. But just *how* dangerous was it? And why? And what was in the chest? Why wouldn't Ma let Grandpa have the key?

The cold shivery feeling wouldn't go away. It stayed like Grandpa's question. The question Ma hadn't answered.

How d'you know he's not in trouble?

CHAPTER 2

Jazzy Shorts

Oliver counted to twenty, waited until he heard Grandpa's boots on the path and then the creak and slam of the shed door, before he went back up the staircase to Ma's room – where tidying was an impossibility. The shopping was more important and Ma insisted on looking after the money. Oliver pushed the door open, climbed over a heap of books, shifted a pile of coloured cottons and knitting off Ma's rocking chair and sat down.

Whenever Oliver looked at Ma, or sat with her, as he did now, Ma grinning at him and him grinning back, he couldn't help but feel pleased and somehow comforted. Ma, with her plump dimpled arms, her frizz of grey and brown hair that refused to obey its many hairpins. Ma, with her impossible clothes that she seemed to wrap or drape about her, adding another layer – shawl, scarf or hat – whatever took her fancy. When Oliver was with her and Ma was in a good mood, it was as if he didn't need to worry about Pa. Didn't need to worry about anything. Only that feeling never lasted. Being with Ma was like basking in sunshine but then discovering that it could turn very chilly. And time after time, week after week, Oliver forgot. Forgot that the sunshine didn't last.

Ma was at her sewing machine. It was an old treadle machine that required Ma to pedal up and down on it with her feet while her hands drew the material under the jab-jab-jab of the needle. The sewing machine was in one corner of the room surrounded by bales of material. There was a row of coloured cottons on a shelf like miniature paint pots. Zips and buttons hung in strips on wobbly hooks.

The rest of the room was taken over with

books on equally wobbly shelves, mostly made out of bricks with planks of wood laid across. Most of the books, to Oliver's shame, bore the mark of a library on their spines. They were organised, as if Ma thought this was *her* library, not a lot of borrowed books, so each shelf had a label. *History, Biography, Art, Philosophy* and so on. From time to time Oliver tried to work out the size of the library fine Ma must owe but it had become too large to even think about.

Finally, Ma gathered up her sewing and sat with it in her lap. 'New trousers,' she said, reaching into her lap and pulling out a pair of long, silky shorts in red, yellow and blue stripes – and was that a fringe at the bottom? 'Jazzy, eh?'

Oliver winced. He was thinking of what the women outside the Stores would say. And even if they didn't actually say anything, he hated the way they looked at him. 'Very jazzy,' he said, wondering if he had a T-shirt long enough to cover them up and if he could cut off the fringe. Oliver could guess, even before trying on the new trousers, that one leg would be shorter than the other. (It was Oliver's notion that Ma did most of her sewing when she was angry which explained why all their clothes were multi-coloured and oddly shaped. Pedalling and jab-jab-jabbing got the temper out of her.)

'They'll be just right for summer,' Ma said comfortably. She herself never left *Dizzy Perch*, complaining of poor circulation in her legs or corns or athlete's foot − though how, Oliver wondered, could anyone get athlete's foot without doing anything more athletic than pedalling a sewing machine? Privately, he thought Ma didn't leave the house because she was waiting for Pa but when he'd once suggested this, Ma had snapped at him. 'The very idea! Quite ridiculous!'

'It's a shopping day,' Oliver said.

'Shopping! Of course it is,' said Ma. 'It must be Wednesday, is it?'

'It is,' said Oliver. 'Potatoes,' he said, 'are you thinking of potatoes?'

'That's it, Dear Thing!' said Ma. 'Potatoes are top of my list.'

Oliver was always trying to find the right moment to ask about Pa and somehow he never got it right. It was puzzling and upsetting and frustrating. Sometimes the mere mention of Pa could put Ma into a tizzy. And that made Oliver feel dim and clumsy, as if he'd done something wrong but didn't know what it was.

The mention of summer seemed like just another opportunity for a question. Oliver tried to slip it in while writing down the shopping list.

'Pasta, yes,' he began. 'And tomatoes and we need more rice and I suppose Pa will be home before summer?'

Ma ignored him, patting a few hairpins back into her frizz and seeming to gaze out of the window. 'I was thinking of sausages,' she said, 'and mash.'

'We had that last night,' said Oliver. 'I was wondering exactly what sort of secret work Pa was busy with?'

(Had Pa become some kind of spy? Was there a dangerous gang somewhere and Pa had been asked to find out what they were up to? And why Pa? Pa was usually good at inventing things. Nice non-dangerous things like a new stain remover or a shampoo that made your hair curly or straight, depending on how you wanted it. Nothing you'd call important. And certainly nothing you'd call secret.)

'What part of the word "secret" do you not understand?' Ma asked. And Oliver knew that somehow he'd trespassed.

'Maybe we could have cottage pie,' he suggested miserably.

Ma fetched some money from the old saucepan where she kept it and handed it to Oliver. Then she went out to her balcony, wrapped herself in several shawls and settled herself in her wicker chair.

'Dear Thing,' called Ma as he was leaving, 'there'll be a parcel of library books for me at the Post Office. Don't forget to collect them.'

'I won't forget,' said Oliver and he stuck his

tongue out at Ma's back. Why, he wondered, were all grown-ups so very confusing, so very mixed up?

There were two ways down to the village of Starwater. If the tide was out you could take the funicular railway down to the beach and, under the shelter of the cliffs, walk along to the harbour. If the tide was in you had to scramble along the rocks until you reached the Creel Road – a grassy path that fishermen once used – and go down to Starwater that way. This was fine going – indeed, Oliver found it more interesting – but it wasn't so fine climbing back again with a rucksack full of shopping and probably library books. Sometimes, depending on the tide, you had to go down one way and back another.

This morning the tide was almost full in which meant that unless your legs were in good working order, *Dizzy Perch* was cut off. Oliver found the quietest pair of shorts he possessed (tartan, but quiet tartan), an old T-shirt and, because it would still be chilly out on the cliffs, one of Ma's knitted jerseys – this one bright blue with a lopsided purple edge and one sleeve longer than the other. Oliver rolled them both up and strapped the rucksack on his back. He didn't bother with shoes. The rocks were easier without them and he liked the feel of the stone and the way it often held the warmth of the sun. Overhead seagulls and guillemots raced across the sky as if they were keeping an eye on him.

It took him half an hour to reach the Creel Road, which was the easy bit, and then he was walking along the row of fishermen's cottages. Seaview Terrace, they were called, which was the right name because they all looked down at the sea and had tidy gardens (each with a washing line) that ran right to the edge of the cliff. There were twelve of them. Oliver loved them, their neatness and friendliness. Their joined-together safety. One or two of the cottages had a bench beside the front door, perhaps for a fisherman to sit and mend his nets and rinse his crabs in a bucket. Not that there were many fishermen left in Starwater.

Oliver walked on down to the harbour heading for the Post Office Stores but, as always, he stopped to see what boats, if any, were in the harbour. There were usually only two, *Exuberant* and *Magnet* – both were out, probably checking their lobster creels. But there was a new one. Oliver tried to read its name. It was an odd name that he couldn't even pronounce. He wrote it down on his arm using the shopping list pen so he could ask Ma or Grandpa about it when he got home. It was *Nadzieja.*

In the Post Office Stores, Mrs Emma Tansley was waiting behind the counter. Oliver knew her name was Emma because it was written across the front of the stores, but he always called her Mrs Tansley and Mrs Tansley always called him Oliver Coggin, as though she enjoyed the name. There was almost nothing you couldn't buy at the stores, from ice cream to whisky, from baked beans to a sack of coal. A side of bacon hung from a hook in the ceiling. There was shelf for newspapers, notebooks, faded birthday cards. Out the back Oliver could glimpse a diver's black wetsuit swaying on a hanger.

When Mrs Tansley had gone through Oliver's list, lining up the items on the counter and then ticking them off, she put on her hat, disappeared under the counter and came up in the front of the Post Office part of the shop. Oliver always thought she looked different in the Post Office. More important, somehow. It was probably the hat that did it. They always began again with Oliver saying, 'Good morning, Mrs Tansley,' and Mrs Tansley saying, 'Good morning, Oliver Coggin.'

And Oliver always asked the same question. He asked it trying to keep the hope out of his face. 'Any letters for Coggin?'

Mrs Tansley always put on her specs and looked in the pigeon hole marked 'C'. Mostly she said, 'Sorry dear, nothing today.' But this morning she said, 'Another parcel of books for your mother. Does she do anything else but read?'

'She sews and knits,' said Oliver defensively.

'I can see that,' said Mrs Tansley, eyeing Oliver's lopsided jersey. 'And there's a card for her from the library.'

'Thank you,' said Oliver. His rucksack was full with potatoes, carrots, a bag of five doughnuts, a loaf of bread, two tins of beans, bananas, tomatoes and a packet of pasta. Mrs Tansley gave him some string and he attached the parcel of books to one strap. He crumpled the card from the library in his pocket. (It was no good taking that home. He'd ditch it on the way.)

Mrs Tansley leaned across the counter. 'How are things up at the Perch?' she asked, curiosity getting the better of her. 'I often wonder how you manage up there.'

'We're fine,' said Oliver. What could he say? That he missed his dad? That no one would answer his questions? That it got very lonely up at *Dizzy Perch*?

'Teach you themselves, do they?' Mrs Tansley asked. 'I expect that's what all these books are about, is it?'

'Yes,' said Oliver. 'They're for our lessons.' (Some of them, he added to himself, but maybe not the romances and Ma's favourite adventure stories.) He hoisted his rucksack – now made much heavier by the dangling parcel of books – on to his back and bought an ice cream cornet for eating on the way.

'See you next week,' said Mrs Tansley. 'If you're not blown away, that is. I hear there's a storm coming.' Oliver could hear her laughing halfway round the harbour.

He sat on the harbour wall to eat his ice cream. The new boat – the one with a funny name – bobbed in the water. It was actually quite an old boat and in need of a coat of paint. But it was new to Starwater. As he watched, a boy came out of the cabin followed by a yappy black-and-white dog. The boy was about Oliver's age and height. He was carrying a paint tin and brush and had obviously begun painting because there were dabs of orange paint in his dark hair. The dog bounced about him as if it was his birthday or Christmas or some other extremely happy occasion.

The boy looked up at Oliver and waved.

Oliver looked away. *Don't talk to strangers*, Ma was always telling them. Did that include boys? Oliver wondered. A boy who might be a friend? Well, it wasn't worth the risk. He slid off the wall and began making his way back towards Seaview Terrace.

Maybe it was just one of those mornings, but there was *another* stranger sitting on the bench beside Starwater's one and only bus stop. Starwater did get the occasional holiday maker, people who wanted to explore the cliffs. Sometimes a diver or two. This man didn't look like either. He had straggly fair hair – rats' tails, Ma would have called them – and wore an old denim jacket, dark green trousers and a bright blue and green scarf. Oliver had a glimpse of scarlet braces under the jacket.

'Morning, son,' he said as Oliver walked by.

Oliver didn't answer. He felt suddenly choked. He was remembering how when he was little Pa had called him 'little man' and then, as he got older, it became 'son'. What a word that was and how Oliver longed to hear it again – but not from a stranger sitting on a bench by a bus stop, even though that stranger had the brightest of blue eyes and a grin that was somehow cheering.

He thought of turning back, just to say hello, but when he looked round the man had vanished. And anyway, the sky was darkening. A troop of gulls came shrieking across the sky as if, like Mrs Tansley, they knew there was a storm coming.

Looking out beyond the harbour Oliver could see *Magnet*, small and brave against the now choppy sea, rounding the cliff and heading for harbour with a froth of wake behind and an escort of hungry gulls in front. The new boat, the one with the funny name, rocked furiously, its thick rope tugging at the bollard on the quay. At the first crack of thunder, the boy and his dog vanished inside the cabin.

CHAPTER 3

Starwater Storm

How quickly the weather could change! Oliver
had reached Seaview Terrace when there was a
slash of lightning, then a roll of thunder, then
another slash of lightning, as if someone was
switching a flashlight on/off, on/off, turning the
whole world strange. For a brief moment
the cottages were lit up, as if for a film set.
Oliver saw an alarmed face in an upstairs
window, heard a front door slam, saw someone
in a cagoul, head bent, hurry inside. He
wondered if he should go back to the Post Office
Stores and wait there until the storm passed
but somehow he didn't want any more questions
from Mrs Tansley.

Maybe someone in the cottages, if he knocked, would allow him to wait there?

Oliver loved the cottages, but he wasn't too sure about the people who lived in them. He might knock and meet one of the women he'd heard saying things. Nasty things about the Coggins being up to no good or hiding something or just being odd. Sometimes when he'd heard them gossiping he'd felt himself about to explode with anger. How dare they talk about his family like that! What did they know saying Grandpa looked like a tramp? Grandpa was grand! So no, he wasn't going to knock on one of the cottage doors and come face to face with one of the Gossips.

He gave a last look down to the harbour, half hoping the boy and his dog would appear, maybe ask him into the boat, but there was no sign of them. The village was deserted. The only person in sight was the man he'd seen at the bus stop. He was just a small distant figure now, his bright stripey blue and green scarf blowing in the wind. Oliver fancied that the man turned and waved and almost instinctively he raised his hand as if to wave back and then thought better of it. The man made him feel uneasy, just hanging about, not doing anything. And somehow that decided him. He'd had enough. He was going home.

The thunder and lightning had stopped. They'd cracked the sky open and now it bucketed down, as if it intended to drown Starwater, batter the cliffs, wash Oliver away. Not to be left out, the wind stirred itself up into a frenzy. Oliver hitched the rucksack up on to his shoulders. He was already soaked through. The sooner he got going the better.

It was far from easy. There was no way he could go back along the beach because the tide was now full in. He could see it down below, lashing the beach. The way back along the cliff meant the wind was in his face and the rain so strong he found it difficult to see. The rocks – so warm and easy on the way – were now dangerously slippy. Rock pools had filled up. Lichen like soggy green sponges got between his toes. The weight of the rucksack bent him over. He untied the parcel of books and squeezed them in on top, hoping they wouldn't crush the doughnuts. Here and there he had to grab hold of some gorse or a clump of grass to avoid falling. The worst part was looking down at the sea. Oliver tried not to. He was remembering what Grandpa said about the month of March. *March comes in like a lion and goes out like a lamb.* Well, this was the lion.

Now, struggling against the wind, trying to keep his footing on the wet rocks, the route that he'd walked how many times – fifty? a hundred? – seemed different. A fitful sun was trying to struggle out from behind the storm clouds. Twice Oliver found himself not on the wrong path, because there wasn't a path, but not on the right, recognisable way.

He tried not to look down at the sea. When he did, it was to see huge, hungry waves leaping up sides of the cliffs. The North Sea, the King Sea, thought Oliver, trying to claim and eat the land. He'd no idea what time it was, only that this had taken him much longer than usual and that his legs ached and he was hungry.

Would anyone come and look for him? Ma probably wouldn't notice he hadn't come back. Lottie and Titch had never been to Starwater on their own. Grandpa? Well, yes if his bad leg wasn't playing up. Now, if Pa was home . . . Oliver shook himself. It was no good thinking like that. Pa *wasn't* home and goodness knows when he would be. Enviously, he thought of the boy down in his boat. He probably had a pa who looked after him. And a ma who didn't have her head in a book all the time. And he wouldn't have a mile long scramble over rocks carrying a load of useless library books. Oliver used the hem of his lopsided jersey to wipe the water from his face. Could you sweat when you were cold and wet? It seemed you could.

With relief, he found himself in sight of *Dizzy Perch.* From this distance, standing there stark against the shifting greys and blacks of the sky, it looked almost unreal. As if he'd imagined it. A voice in his head seemed to say, *This is no place for children*. And then all the other Coggin voices seemed to answer him.

It's like living with the birds – Grandpa.

You get to understand the weather up here – Ma.

It's our magic place – Titch.

I'm the luckiest person in the world – Lottie.

And of course they were right. *Dizzy Perch was* magical and wonderful and they were exceptionally lucky and that lonely ache he often felt had nothing to do with the house. It was inside him.

As if the weather – or maybe *Dizzy Perch* itself – had heard him, the rain stopped. The wind dropped. Sunshine pushed aside the dark clouds and, as he climbed the last rocks, very faintly came the sound of a fiddle. Grandpa! Out on his balcony, doing what he called *addressing the weather with music.* Oliver smiled. And just as he reached the steps that led up to the back door, two small figures rushed out and swamped him in hugs. Oliver dropped the rucksack to take on the weight of Lottie flinging herself at him and Titch stopping all movement by wrapping his arms round Oliver's legs.

'We thought you were lost in the storm . . .' said Lottie.

'And maybe drowned,' said Titch, swallowing a sob.

'We missed you,' said Lottie.

'Thought you wouldn't come home,' Titch sniffed.

'Sillies!' said Oliver, letting Lottie down and hoisting Titch on to his hip, and thinking how good it was to feel missed.

'I'll always come home,' he said. Was that what Pa had said when he left? Oliver found he couldn't remember. What if Pa never came home? He shoved the thought away. 'Anyone fancy a doughnut?' he asked.

The question was enough to set both of them squealing and running into the kitchen.

'You can find them while I go and get dry,' said Oliver, dumping the rucksack on the kitchen floor for Lottie and Titch to unzip it and start rummaging.

He dripped his way up the spiral staircase, stripped off in the bathroom and found some dry clothes – the new and awful silky striped shorts and a shirt with an embroidered dragon on the back. There was nothing else. As usual, Ma had forgotten to do the washing. Actually, Ma preferred to sew new clothes out of her unending basket of old curtains, recyclable shirts, patched skirts, than do any washing. With a sigh, Oliver thought he'd better do it himself if he didn't want to stay in these awful stripy shorts for weeks.

Down in the kitchen, Lottie had put away the shopping, veg in the vegetable tray, tins in the big cupboard, bread in the bread bin, bananas in a bowl. Titch had set the doughnuts on a plate and, with his elbows on the table and his head on his arms, was gazing at them. They were rather squashed but that only made the insides nice and oozy.

'There's five,' Titch said. 'Three jam and two

lemon curd. And I've waited for you.'

'One for each of us,' said Oliver and he put two aside for Ma and Grandpa.

'If they don't want theirs . . .' said Titch hopefully.

'They will,' said Lottie.

She was right, of course. Only a sense of fairness made Oliver go back up to Ma's room with a doughnut, a cup of tea and the parcel of library books.

'Why, Dear Thing!' exclaimed Ma. 'I'd quite forgotten you'd gone shopping. And don't you look a picture in those new trousers. Give Ma a kiss now.'

Oliver obliged, pecking Ma on the cheek.

'There was a storm,' he said, for at least Ma should know the trouble he'd gone to, getting the shopping done and struggling back in the wind and the rain.

'So there was,' said Ma. 'I had to shut the door of the balcony it was blowing such a gale.'

'I got very wet,' said Oliver.

'Did you, Dear Thing?' said Ma. 'Oh. A lovely

doughnut and lovelier books. Let's see what we've got.' Ma used her dressmaking scissors to open the parcel.

Oliver perched on the window sill. There were five books. 'Three for lessons, two for me,' said Ma. She handed the lesson books to Oliver. There was *Mathematics Explained*, *Get Into Medical School* and *Jolly Phonics*. 'That one's for Titch,' Ma said.

'He doesn't need it,' said Oliver. 'Grandpa's taught him to read. And why did you order *Get Into Medical School?*'

'Well, you never know,' said Ma. 'One of you might want to go to medical school one day. An education should be as broad as possible.'

Ma's own books were *Love at Last* and *Adventure in the Rockies*. Ma put them beside her bed.

Oliver suddenly remembered that ever since Ma and Grandpa had begun home schooling, Ma had collected all manner of encyclopedias and dictionaries.

'There was a new boat in the harbour,' he

said. 'I wrote its name down on my arm. But it's probably washed away.'

He pulled up his sleeve. The word was still there, if a little runny. He showed it to Ma. *Nadzieja.*

'Sounds Russian. Or Czech. Or Polish,' said Ma. She had got herself very sticky on the doughnut. Oliver waited. She didn't cook. She didn't do the washing. She bought ridiculous books. He loved her.

'Third time lucky,' said Ma. 'It's Polish. It means *Hope.*'

Oliver left the last doughnut outside Grandpa's door. He'd knocked.

'I'm out,' said Grandpa.

'Doughnut,' said Oliver.

'Maybe I'm in,' said Grandpa. A wrinkly old hand reached out. A doughnut vanished. Oliver grinned.

CHAPTER 4

The Stranger

In the morning, Oliver found Ma sitting out on her balcony, tucked up in rugs, *Love at Last* on her lap.

'I've come for the washing,' Oliver said. Looking out of Ma's window he was suddenly struck by the magnificence of the view. Almost, he thought, like world's end – that point where the sea met the sky, world's end or another world nobody ever reached. Perhaps it was unkind to think that Ma was just lazy. Perhaps she sat up here reading (or sewing) and watching and waiting for Pa. Maybe watching and waiting was very important. Maybe it was almost a kind of prayer.

He went back into her bedroom and began

gathering up large nighties, skirts and shirts, the sheets from last week, any number of socks, one flowery shawl, knickers. Most of it was under the bed, some of it had strayed into dusty corners of the room. Sometimes it was hard to tell what was an item to be washed and what was a piece of material Ma was about to turn into something.

It was as Oliver was making a pile of it all that his eye was caught by something glinting. And then he saw it! How could he *not* have seen it before? The key. It hung on a hook of its own and you didn't notice it because it was just one hook among lots of hooks, all of them dangling with scissors, poppers, zips. Your eye just didn't see it. But it was definitely the key to the chest in Pa's room. The key that might tell him where Pa was. The key Grandpa wanted. There were things about Pa that Grandpa knew. Oliver could tell by the way Grandpa often went suddenly quiet whenever the subject of Pa came up, that there were things Grandpa wanted to say but couldn't. He'd open his mouth as if about to begin then Ma would give him one of her fierce looks and Grandpa would clamp his mouth shut and slope off.

Oliver stood there with his arms full of washing. He could just take it. Now. Quickly. In his pocket in a flash. He heard the creak of Ma's wicker chair as she got up. He heard her gathering up her books, tugging the rugs round her. She'd be back in the room in minutes . . .

Oliver hesitated. Should he take it now, while it was there, glinting at him! *Wanting* to be taken! Flashes of the conversation between Ma and Grandpa echoed in his head.

If you'd just let me have the key at least we'd know where *he was even if we didn't know* how *he was* – Grandpa.

He doesn't want us to know where he is – Ma.

How d'you know he's not in trouble? – Grandpa.

Ma had promised not to open the chest. But it wouldn't be Ma, would it? It would be him, Oliver. What would Pa want him to do? That was the important question. To take the key would be stealing wouldn't it?

Ma was coming through from the balcony. *I can wait*, thought Oliver. *Now I know where the key is kept, I can wait. I can get it another time.* It would be easy. And it wouldn't be stealing, he told himself. It would just be borrowing.

It was a fine, windy day. The sort of day that made hanging out the washing a delight. Particularly when you've a whole beach to yourself, a washing line strung between a tree and a stump and just to begin you have to ride down on the funicular railway.

There was a lever for the funicular at the front door. It was heavy and quite stiff but all the Coggins had learnt how to turn it ever so gently one notch until the wires started to hum. Then you listened until you were sure they were going smoothly and turned the lever another notch. Two old bucket seats rode up, each with a belt that you fixed across your tum, as if, as Titch often said, you were in an aeroplane waiting for take-off. How did Titch know this, Oliver had asked him. 'Pa told me,' Titch said.

Oliver settled the basket of washing into one of the two bucket seats and himself in the other. One last notch of the lever and he and the washing were on their way. Now and again the ride was a little jerky – particularly if it had been raining – but mostly it was a smooth ride. There was something almost kingly about sailing down the side of the cliff in your very own funicular railway, thought Oliver.

How many boys had a dad who could make a funicular railway? he asked out loud, as he sailed down to the beach. Pa had made it from all manner of odds and ends, bus seats, iron bars, a wheel or two and some chains. If only there was someone to show it to. Someone his own age. He thought of the boy in the harbour and how good it would be to bring him here and show off, just a little – to say, 'My dad made this! Like a ride?'

He got off the funicular, remembering to switch the lock beneath both bucket seats and to turn the dial to OFF before he took the basket and set it down. There was a ridge at the top of the beach that almost shone with sea-smoothed pebbles mixed with crushed white shells like so much broken crockery. (This was Titch's favourite place for collecting sea glass and stones.) There were a few rock pools with strands of seaweed, an occasional tuft of pale pink thrift and then sand. Miles of sand formed a bay with caves burrowing back into the cliffs and a few sheltered places if you wanted to swim and sunbathe.

It would have been fairly easy for people to walk from Starwater to this beach but they didn't. There was an easy beach on the other side of the harbour. Oliver had to admit that it was somehow friendlier. You could see houses. If you walked up the hill a bit there was a café that sometimes opened in summer. And you could always get a bottle of lemonade or an ice cream from the Post Office Stores. Here there was nothing but rocks and caves and *Dizzy Perch* looking down at you. Oliver had heard the old men in the village say that there were lots of tales about the house – even that it was haunted. Oliver would have liked to hear some of the tales. If they existed. (Was *Dizzy Perch* haunted? At night the house creaked and groaned so much it would have been hard to hear a ghost. If there was one.)

Oliver began hanging out the washing. He should have brought Titch with him to hand up the pegs. The wind kept tugging Grandpa's nightshirt away before he could get it firmly pegged. He had to chase after Lottie's skirt which was so flimsy that it flew across some rocks, tangled with some seaweed and almost landed in a rock pool. Eventually he had all the clothes out, dancing on the line, rather like cheerful ghosts, Oliver thought, as the arms of Grandpa's nightshirt waved at him and Lottie's skirt curtsied up and down.

Oliver put the empty basket back in the bucket seat, turned the dial to ON, sat himself in the other seat and waited for the jerk and shudder that set the funicular going up. He was halfway up the cliff when he saw him, the man from the harbour bus stop, strolling along the beach with his green trouser bottoms rolled up and carrying his shoes in his hand.

Oliver almost fell out of the bucket seat straining to look at him. Was he looking up at *Dizzy Perch*? Oliver couldn't see. He was glad when the funicular reached the top and he could scramble out, move the big lever to nought and make sure the funicular was completely silent.

From up the top, the man was out of sight. Perhaps he'd put his shoes back on and was walking along the ridge of pebbles and shells. Hopefully he was going back to Starwater. Should he tell Ma and Grandpa about him? No. There was no point in alarming them. Oliver went back to the kitchen for the second load of washing. He thought he'd hang this lot on the kitchen clothes horse, mostly used in winter. He didn't want to risk going down to the beach and finding the stranger still there, and looking up at *Dizzy Perch*.

Oliver folded the washing into the laundry basket, wondering who the man was who'd called him 'son'. He wished now that he'd said hello to the stranger. Found out who he was, even. Too late now. And why oh why hadn't he taken the key to the chest? It was glinting at him! Wanting to be taken! He was a fool not to have seized the moment. What was it Grandpa had said to Ma? If you'd just let me have the key at least we'd know where he was even if we didn't know how he was. So what hope did he, Oliver, have of knowing either where or how Pa was unless he got hold of the key?

Somehow or other he'd have to do it. Find the right moment – and the courage – to borrow the key from Ma. Borrow? He'd have to keep reminding himself that that's what he was going to do. Borrow. Not steal. That was a better word. Borrow. And then what?

Well, when he'd found out what was in the chest, he'd do whatever it took to find his pa.

CHAPTER 5

A Key and a Cure

All the following week Oliver tried to work out how he was going to sneak into Ma's room and borrow/steal the key. He worried about it while he was cooking. And he slept badly, tossing, and turning, counting the possibilities. He could listen out for when Ma went to talk to Grandpa in Grandpa's room. He could creep in when she was having her afternoon nap – forty winks she called it, though it lasted a lot longer. Or even at night. But there wasn't a door in Dizzy Perch that didn't creak or rattle. Ma's did both. And in any case, Ma's forty winks seemed to be all the sleep she needed. She had a habit of wandering the house at night in her silky dressing gown, woolly shawl and soft, shuffly slippers. Sometimes she'd raid the kitchen, make herself a nice fat sandwich. Sometimes Grandpa joined her. Oliver had often been lulled to sleep by the murmur of their voices in the kitchen. Hearing them made the night less lonely.

And nights in *Dizzy Perch were* lonely. When all you could see was stars sharp in the dark and the moon edging the waves with silver, and all you could hear was the sea slapping at the cliffs or the occasional late cry of gull or gannet, maybe even an owl, hooting far across the cliffs, then you felt a long way from anywhere. And anyone. Oliver was glad when Biggles the cat curled up on the bottom of his bed. Glad too, when he heard the soft hiss of Ma's silk dressing gown or the sound of her shuffly slippers padding round the house. Once, coming barefoot down stairs to the toilet, he'd heard her go into Pa's study and shut the door behind her. He'd wondered how long she'd sat there, with the always open shutters, maybe sitting in the swivel chair at Pa's desk, but looking out to sea.

His chance came one Lesson Morning. Lessons were a fairly haphazard event at *Dizzy Perch*. All three of them preferred Grandpa's lessons to Ma's because Grandpa took them out exploring while Ma's lessons came out of a book. At least, as Lottie often said, the book was a surprise. Ma didn't seem to believe in starting a subject at the beginning and going on to the end. Ma's theory of education was a bit of this and a bit of that. Battles, for instance. (They'd done Agincourt and Bannockburn.) A hero or heroine. (They'd done Sir Francis Drake and Grace Darling). Relativity. (This had been a struggle.) Ma called it 'whetting your appetites for knowledge' and mostly it worked because they were always left wanting more.

'But what happened to Grace Darling in the end?' – Lottie.

'Was Sir Isaac really hit on the head by an apple? – Titch.

Then Ma would point to the Encyclopaedia and tell them to look it up for themselves, though mostly they forgot.

Ma's lessons were often conducted from her bed, with all three of them gathered round her on the floor. But sometimes, as that morning, a note had gone to each of them. *This morning's lesson will be in the sitting room at ten o'clock. Subject: Biology.*

'That's the body,' said Titch, feeling rather clever. He'd already peeped into the sitting room and reported that there was a plastic skeleton hanging on the wall.

'And there's a poster about human body parts,' said Lottie.

'This is all about *Getting Into Medical School*,' said Oliver. 'It's the latest book from the library.'

'Sounds good,' said Lottie. 'I'll go and get dressed for it.'

Dressing up was what Lottie liked doing most of all.

'She likes it more than eating,' Titch said, though this wasn't quite true.

When she could, Lottie liked to dress in keeping with whatever lesson Ma had planned.

Ma encouraged this. She called it 'participating'. Oliver called it 'messing about'.

So when Ma arrived at the sitting room, *Getting Into Medical School* under her arm, there was already a notice on the door saying *Dr Lott's Surgery* and there was Lottie in a (mostly) white coat and with a stethoscope round her neck and there was Titch with a bandage round his head that was slipping down over his nose.

'Ah,' said Ma, 'that's what I like to see. Imaginative play.'

'Lie down here, please, I need to listen to your heart,' said Lottie, pointing to the sofa.

'Dear Thing!' said Ma, doing as she was told. 'The heart is the organ that circulates the blood. It pumps it to all parts of . . .'

'Quiet, please,' said Dr Lott applying her stethoscope. 'I need to listen. I think your heart's stopped.'

'Rubbish!' said Ma.

'Let me listen! Let me listen too!' cried Titch.

'There's nothing wrong with my heart,' said

Ma fretfully.

'All right. I'll just put a bandage round your ankle,' said Dr Lott. 'I think you might have fractured it.'

'All the bones of the body . . .' Ma began.

But Oliver used the moment to slip out of the 'surgery' and run up the stairs to Ma's room. She'd left her door open so he didn't have to worry about creaks or rattles. As usual the room was a chaos of sewing stuffs and books. And why was she always telling them to make their beds when she never seemed to make her own? Biggles was snoozing in a nest of duvet. He looked up indignantly when Oliver appeared.

All the Coggins loved Biggles. They loved his smooth, sleek, ginger fur. They loved the white blobs on his very fine tail and the matching white blobs on the tips of his ears. They all admired his long twitchy whiskers. When he wasn't prowling round *Dizzy Perch* as if hunting for trespassers, Biggles liked chasing cotton reels with Lottie, or supervising Oliver's cooking, or purring in time to Grandpa's fiddle and waving his tail in time to the music or finding a nice patch of sunshine to lie in on Grandpa's workbench.

Oliver went straight to the wall by the sewing machine where all the zips and scissors hung, above them the shelf of bright cotton reels. But somehow the key didn't shine out at him. Oliver counted the hooks. Had it been the third hook along? The fifth? Was it between the blue zip and the scissors with purple handles?

In despair Oliver plumped down on the bed. (Biggles scooted away.) It was no good counting. It was no good looking. Ma had moved the key. Oliver was close to tears. He felt so miserable and cross he would have liked to turn Ma's room upside down and inside out but it already was that way. Besides, he couldn't risk Ma knowing he'd been looking for the key.

From downstairs he could hear Titch calling him – 'Olly! Olly! It's your turn. I've just had an operation. Don't worry, I'm all better now.' When Oliver went back into the sitting room he found Titch dancing with the skeleton –

Titch's feet tapping, the skeleton's plastic bones clacking, Ma clapping.

Oliver slumped sulkily on the second sofa.

'It's medicine time!' declared Dr Lott. 'Line up!'

On the table was a row of small bottles with greenish coloured stuff inside.

'This is Wondicure,' said Dr Lott, shaking one up so you could see unpleasant black blobs in it. 'It will cure anything.'

'Dear Thing,' said Ma. 'Maybe you're going to be like your father, and discover all kinds of wonderful things.'

'If she did that, she'd go away like Pa, and never come home,' said Titch, his lower lip trembling.

'Nonsense!' said Ma.

'Wondicare could make you all beautifully thin,' said Dr Lott, 'for when Pa *does* come home.'

'Whenever that is . . .' Oliver muttered.

'Dear Things!' said Ma, as if suddenly feeling got at, 'Pa loves me just as I am – not quite thin, not quite fat. Nicely in-between.'

'Wondicare works wonders!' announced Dr Lott, feeling rather proud of her slogan. 'This will cheer you up, Olly.'

Oliver unslumped himself and stood up. 'I don't want cheering up!' he shouted.

'He just wants Pa,' said Titch, trying and failing to give Oliver a hug. (Oliver shrugged him off.)

'And I don't want your yucky medicine,' he continued. 'And I'm nobody's Dear Thing!'

He wanted only to be away – away from *Dizzy Perch*, away just to clear his head, to be not a Dear Thing, not a big brother, not Olly who looked after everyone and did the cooking and the shopping and the cleaning, but just to be himself, Oliver Coggin.

'Keep your hair on!' said Dr Lott, looking a little tearful.

'It is on!' said Oliver. 'And hair is the only thing we all have in common!' And shaking his own ginger mop at all of them, he slammed out of the room.

'Maybe you need a brain transplant!' Dr Lott shouted after him.

'Poor boy. Dear Thing!' said Ma comfortably, as if certain her endearment would make everything better.

But if Oliver heard, he didn't answer. He was away out, over the rocks, taking deep breaths of the fresh, sea-salty air, sure-footed and nimble, jumping puddles, easy on the ups and downs, heading for Starwater.

CHAPTER 6

Finding a Friend

It was perhaps just a freak of the weather, but it seemed to Oliver that a swirl of mist surrounded *Dizzy Perch* while Starwater was bathed in sunshine. March was crossed off the kitchen calendar. April was new and showery – perhaps that was why the mist was slow to lift off *Dizzy Perch.* But you couldn't help knowing that a new month had arrived.

It was mid-morning and even among the birds there was a busyness. Out at sea Oliver could see the funny bath-duck shape of puffins returning early. Soon they'd be looking for nesting places in the cliffs and gullies. Up high, gannets were watching. Herring gulls yowled at each other or at life. The cliffs themselves were beginning to grow their own hair – not ginger of course, but dark green with pads of lichen soft as fur and sharp grass, fresh as new green apples.

Starting up, Oliver thought. Everything is starting up.

It was even more obvious along the Creel Path. Poppies had arrived. All the grasses – timothy, meadow barley, wild oats – seemed to be quivering with new life, tickling his legs as he hurried along, feeling as if he'd caught it, this new spring energy that was making everything burst into life. He hurried on towards the harbour. Seeing the boats always made him think of adventures, of worlds beyond *Dizzy Perch* and Starwater.

All three boats – *Exuberant*, *Magnet* and *Nadzieja* – were in. Oliver remembered that Ma had told him that *Nadzieja* was the Polish word for *hope*. What was a boat with a Polish name doing in Starwater? Right now he found himself hoping he might see the boy again, the boy who'd waved at him. Oliver hadn't waved back, but the picture of the boy jumping out of the boat followed by the yappy black-and-white dog had stayed in his mind. It came to him suddenly that he was hoping for a friend.

Oliver knew all the boats would have been out, probably at dawn, to collect their lobsters and crabs from the pots and creels set out for them in the places the fishermen knew best. *Exuberant* looked like its name, bright and cheerful with its yellow funnel and a matching stripe round its bow. It bobbed on its anchor as if pleased to be home. Its owner was out on the quay, sorting out his nets, a box of lobsters beside him, their claws stilled. The net was a tangle of seaweeds and slime. The fisherman's hands were large but deft. Soon he'd got rid of all the sea debris, and had hung them to dry on the sea-wall held down by a few stones, and was off up home. It would be breakfast or lunch, thought Oliver, or maybe a combination.

There was no sign of *Magnet's* man. Perhaps he'd done for the day. Oliver hurried. If the boy wasn't with the boat, he had no idea where he lived. Maybe one of the cottages of Seaview Terrace. Mrs Tansley might know, but Oliver was shy of asking.

Then he didn't have to! Just as he reached the harbour wall, out of the boat – jumping out like hope itself – came the black-and-white dog, shaking itself all over so that its fur looked static. Then it went prancing in circles, its plume of a tail working like a flag as if to announce that it was really a landlubber and very glad to have four paws on land. He made Oliver smile.

After him, climbing out, came the boy, a cap of dark hair, long brown legs, a T-shirt with something foreign written on it, a bucket of crabs in his hand. He dumped the bucket on the quay, looked up, saw Oliver, smiled and waved.

Oliver felt a jolt of happiness go through him. Without a moment's hesitation, forgetting all about Ma's injunctions about not talking to strangers – well, this boy really couldn't count as a stranger, could he? – Oliver waved back.

His smile faded a little as after the boy, a man climbed out of the boat. He was wearing yellow oilskin trousers with braces over a rough purple jersey. He had the same dark hair as the boy but dabbed with grey and the same brown eyes and wide mouth. He stood on the quay taking off his oilskins while the dog danced about both of them. Father and son, Oliver realised as the pair of them began making their way up to Starwater's main street (such as it was), the father with an arm slung casually about his son. (Oliver felt an ache of jealousy.)

When they reached the harbour entrance they both stopped. The man said something to the boy as if giving him permission, slapped him on the shoulder and went off on his own. The dog hesitated as if uncertain who to stay with and decided on the boy.

Together, as if they'd agreed on it, Oliver and the boy hoisted themselves up onto the harbour wall, their legs dangling over the side.

'I see you here before,' the boy said. 'I wave

but you don't wave back.' He spoke English slowly, carefully. 'Maybe you shy.'

'I had to get home,' Oliver said, damned if he was going to admit to feeling shy.

'I think maybe we are same age,' said the boy. Then he laughed. 'But from different countries!'

'Yes,' said Oliver, grinning back at him. 'I'm from here. From Scotland. I'm Oliver.' Oliver held out his hand.

'And I'm Cezary. And I'm from Poland.' He pointed to his T-shirt. It said *GDANSK*. 'That's where I'm from,' said Cezary.

'And the dog?' asked Oliver.

'The dog is from here. We found him how d'you say? With nobody.'

'Stray,' said Oliver.

'So we call him *Cheerio*. Because he is cheerful, yes?'

'Sort of,' said Oliver. 'And sometimes it means goodbye.'

'But you and I say hello.'

'We do,' said Oliver.

'But you don't live in the village. I don't see you every day. Only now and sometimes.'

'I live up there,' said Oliver pointing up the cliffs. He felt extraordinarily pleased that Cezary had been looking out for him.

'You live in the clouds?'

Oliver laughed. 'There is a house there. Really. It's called *Dizzy Perch*.'

'Like a castle,' said Cezary. 'You very lucky.'

'Not really like a castle,' said Oliver, though he supposed that Lottie's tower did make *Dizzy Perch* look a bit like a castle.

'I live here,' said Cezary. 'We rent cottage. Number 3 Seaview Terrace. You can see it from here. Me and my ma and pa.'

Oliver felt the same quick stab of jealousy.

'But the others are missing,' Cezary continued.

'The others?'

'Yes. I have two brothers and small sister. We try to earn money to bring them from Poland. It is very difficult.'

'I know about missing,' said Oliver slowly.

He looked at Cezary's friendly, open face. He was about to say that it was his pa who was missing. His pa who was on important, secret work which is why they didn't know where he was. But then he heard Ma's voice in his head. *What part of the word 'secret' don't you understand?* she was saying. He swallowed hard. Shut the words off. He'd been about to tell! About Pa being a scientist and making important discoveries. Possibly dangerous ones. Horrors! If Pa was kidnapped or tied up somewhere it could have been all his, Oliver's, fault. No, he mustn't talk. Not yet. Not unless it felt safe.

'We shall be friends,' Cezary was saying. 'I come to see you in your Perch.'

'Maybe,' said Oliver. He'd have to clear it with Ma, he was thinking. And then what would Cezary make of his Ma with all her books and Grandpa with his fiddle, and Lottie who might be dressed as a doctor or a cowboy or mermaid and Titch who might well be dancing? And then did he want to share Cezary with the rest of the

71

Coggins, or did he want to keep him for himself? His special friend. His only friend.

'I'll see you here,' Oliver said. 'Soon.'

Cezary shrugged. 'Soon. Yes,' he said and slid off the wall. 'Now I go home.'

Oliver watched him running up towards Seaview Terrace with Cheerio bounding after him. Then he began his own homeward journey. The tide was out. It meant he could walk back along the beach.

He'd just turned down the road below the harbour when he saw him again. The stranger. Or was it? This time he was on a motorbike. Oliver could see the straggly fair hair jutting out beneath the man's helmet. He was gone before Oliver could be certain, roaring round the corner. And was that a wave?

CHAPTER 7

Ghosts

It was good walking back along the beach. Bare feet on the cool, flat sand, the tide far out like a rolled-up blanket waiting for someone to fling it out on the bed of the beach, the sky sorting out the clouds like so many pillows and the gulls wheeling overhead, screeching mysteriously urgent messages.

Oliver was cheered. So all right, it was mid April and Pa still wasn't home. (Using last year's calendar, Oliver had counted the weeks since Pa had left in October. They totalled twenty-seven. How many days was that? He hadn't worked it out.) Seeing Cezary's pa putting his arm round his son, as if loving was as natural as breathing, made Oliver ache even to think about it. But hey, he had a new friend. And there was no need to give up, was there? Ma had moved the key to the chest but he could keep looking couldn't he? Dimly he remembered Pa helping him make pancakes and how they'd got it wrong and made them all sloppy and Pa had said, *If at first you don't succeed, try, try again*. And they had, and they'd been even worse and Pa had laughed and said, *And again!*

So that was it, wasn't it? He'd try again. Oliver danced along the beach wishing he had a waggy Cheerio to dance or prance with him. And it was as if the idea had come to him out of the sky like a feather fallen from a seagull and it was so obvious that he must be an idiot not to have thought of it before.

Grandpa! He needed Grandpa's help. Together, he and Grandpa could talk Ma round. Of course it meant confessing that he'd been listening in to him and Ma talking and Grandpa wouldn't be pleased about that! There were some things Grandpa was really strict about.

They mostly came under the label of Good Manners. Oliver knew, without asking, that eavesdropping on other people's conversations was certainly not good manners. He'd have to take a deep breath and say a lot of sorries.

Now that Oliver was thinking about it, he could picture the way Grandpa drooped as he walked away, his shoulders sagging, his bad leg seeming to drag more than usual. It dawned on Oliver with that kind of amazing surprise that often accompanies a new idea, that Grandpa was missing Pa just as much as he, Oliver, was. Of course he was! Pa was Grandpa's son. What father wanted his son to go missing? Oliver hurried. All he had to do was to find Grandpa in the right mood.

Oliver hurried. He reached the base of the funicular railway, unbolted the gate at the bottom and danged the bell so that someone up above – most likely Titch (who liked doing it) or Lottie (who mostly couldn't be bothered to come down from her tower) would switch it on and send down one of the bucket seats.

After several minutes he heard the familiar cranking noise and then the smooth buzz as a bucket seat slid down to fetch him. He could just see Titch's head at the top. 'Thanks, Titch!' he shouted, and sailed up the cliff side with his spirits suddenly as high as the cliffs on which *Dizzy Perch* was perched.

He had to wait until the evening to talk to Grandpa. Most of the day Grandpa was in his workshop and disturbing him there was not a good idea. At least half of the furniture in *Dizzy Perch* had been made by Grandpa and nowadays there always seemed to be something that needed mending. The leg of a chair, a broken handle, some coat hooks that had fallen down, a cupboard door that had fallen off its hinges. When he had the time, Grandpa liked carving animals. There were lots of them about the house – mostly wild animals – camels and tigers and elephants. Ma called them *Grandpa's Zoo*, rather as if Grandpa was a child (or even a Dear Thing) like Oliver, Titch and Lottie. But Oliver thought Grandpa's animals were rather beautiful. Grandpa had given each of them an animal at Christmas. Titch had got a monkey, Lottie, a very elegant giraffe and Oliver a lion because Grandpa said 'a first son needs to be brave as'.

Oliver thought of this, stroking the lion that stood on his windowsill, as he waited for the evening when he could talk to Grandpa in his room. Even then, it was hard to pick the right moment.

Oliver cooked a very special supper in the hope of putting everyone – but particularly Grandpa – in a good mood. Sausages and mash and baked beans was one of Grandpa's favourites. Oliver made sure the mash was well and truly mashed. He added lots of milk and butter. Grandpa also had a very sweet tooth. Oliver decided on a large apple and sultana crumble. He stewed the apples. Then in a big bowl he mixed together flour, butter and sugar, rubbing the first two through his fingers until they made a crumble and then adding the sugar. Afterwards, his fingers were nicely lickable.

When it came out of the oven crisply browned, he dusted the top with icing sugar. It looked so good, he could hardly resist trying a spoonful or two himself. He found a last tin of ginger beer in the cupboard and put it beside Grandpa's place. Everyone else could have water. Even Ma said this was one of Oliver's very best suppers.

Grandpa had two helpings of crumble, drank all his ginger beer, ruffled Oliver's hair and said, 'Thank you kindly, young man.' Then he went to his room and fell fast asleep. They could hear his snores two floors down.

With a sigh Oliver cleared the table and washed the dishes.

'Dear Thing!' said Ma, going away with the book she'd been reading under the table.

Oliver hung about in the sitting room. Then he played about on the spiral staircase. (Mostly he'd given up doing this. It was something all the Coggin children liked doing, swinging round and round the curly rail then jumping off.) Doing it allowed him to listen in to Grandpa. A list of questions was growing in his head. Did

Grandpa have any idea what Pa was doing? Might they both persuade Ma to let them look in the chest? Did Grandpa know where Ma kept the key? And importantly, should he tell Grandpa about Cezary? It would be nice to tell someone, he thought. And if not Grandpa, who?

Ma would fuss. Lottie would be very nosy and want to have Cezary for her friend. Titch then? But Titch simply couldn't keep a secret. So maybe Grandpa, but not just yet.

After a while Grandpa's snores stopped. Instead, Grandpa began talking. Oliver could hear him moving about in his room, talking as he walked.

'Grandpa's talking to his ghosts again,' said Titch, climbing over Oliver and carrying a new bag of pebbles to his room. 'He's had too much pudding.'

Oliver pinched Titch's bottom. Titch poked a tongue at him by way of a reply and hopped out of the way.

They were all used to Grandpa's ghosts. 'It's because Grandpa's very old,' Ma had explained, 'and when you're very old you have real friends and ghost friends. The ghost friends are the ones who've died but you don't forget them and they don't forget you. They become a bit like characters in a book.'

This last notion seemed to please Ma. Oliver was less certain. Sometimes he wondered if Ma could tell the difference between people in a book, real people and now Grandpa's ghosts.

Sometimes, when there was nothing better to do in winter time, when they were tired of all the games from the sitting room cupboard – *Pictionary*, *Frustration*, *Charades*, *Monopoly*, *Scrabble* – the Coggins lined up on the spiral staircase to listen to Grandpa talking to his ghosts. They got to know them.

'He's talking about steam engines,' Titch would say.

'That must be his old pal, Big Jim,' Ma replied. 'He and Grandpa were very keen on steam engines.'

Sometimes they'd hear Grandpa talking in a low, tender voice. Then he'd play his fiddle and sing a love song. 'Ah, he's singing to Grandma Coggin,' Ma would say and that always made Lottie cry.

Mostly you could tell how Grandpa was feeling by the tunes he played. Oliver's favourites were cheerful kinds of jigs that made Titch dance. Lately there'd been melancholy tunes. Tunes that wound around your heart and made you feel sad without knowing why.

Everyone else had gone to bed and Oliver himself was almost falling asleep, just sitting on the cold iron step and leaning his head on a cushion he'd fetched from the sitting room. He was almost about to give up and try another day or night when the door opened and out came Grandpa in his pyjamas and dressing gown, a milk jug in his hand, looking happy and peaceful which was how he always looked when he'd spent an evening with his ghosts.

'Hello, young man,' said Grandpa. 'What are you doing out here? I'm just about to make some hot chocolate. Want some?'

Oliver jumped to his feet. 'I'll get some milk for you,' he said, taking the milk jug.

'Thank you kindly,' said Grandpa. 'I don't suppose there's any of that wonderful crumble left, is there?'

'No,' said Oliver.

'Then we'll have to make do with biscuits,' said Grandpa.

Because Grandpa's room, like Oliver's, was on the same side as the spiral staircase, both rooms were smaller than Ma's and Titch's. But Oliver loved being in Grandpa's room not only because of the small camping stove (on which Grandpa now boiled up the milk and stirred it into the chocolate, so that you felt as if you were a very special guest), but also because the photographs placed all round the walls – some large, some small, some in silver frames, some in fine old oval frames – made you feel as if you'd come into another world, a world full not only of ghosts but of memories and stories. It was in here, looking at a photograph of Grandpa as a boy, or Grandpa and Grandma on their wedding day or Grandpa with a young boy beside him – well, surely Pa at just about Oliver's age? – that Oliver suddenly felt as if he belonged to something big and long-ago and now, all at once. And it was a good feeling, as warm as the hot chocolate.

Once they each had a mug, Grandpa settled in his leather chair with lots of squashy cushions behind him and a stool for his poorly leg while Oliver curled up on the bed. Down below them, far down below *Dizzy Perch*, the sea hushed up the beach, hushed and drew back, hushed and drew back. A gap in Grandpa's curtains showed a thin moon looking in at them.

'I think you've important things to say,' said Grandpa, searching Oliver's face.

'Yes,' said Oliver, screwing his hands together, for how to begin?

'Sometimes important things are hard to say,' suggested Grandpa. 'Maybe begin at the beginning.'

So Oliver began. He told how he'd overhead Grandpa and Ma talking. How Grandpa had worried about Pa being in trouble or in danger. Kidnapped even. (Oliver's voice broke a little at that point.) How he heard them talking about the chest in Pa's study and Ma refusing to let Grandpa look in it even though it might at least let them know where Pa was. And anyway, what could Pa be doing? Didn't he care for them any more? Nothing was quite right without Pa. Other boys had a Pa who stayed at home. Why wasn't he here for Christmas? Or Lottie's birthday? Had Grandpa looked at the calendar lately? Days and days had gone by. Oliver had crossed them off, and no Pa.

It all came tumbling out. The faster Oliver talked, the wilder he got, until the tears were running down his cheeks and he had to rub them away with his fists and Grandpa sat and waited and listened until Oliver ran out of words and stopped like a bus that had run out of petrol.

'And I'm sorry, Grandpa,' Oliver finished, 'about listening in. And I know I shouldn't but you see nobody tells me anything and I'm old enough to be told and it's horrible not knowing and maybe you . . . maybe you and me together . . . could persuade Ma to let us look in the chest, maybe even we could go and find Pa . . .' Oliver's voice tailed off because Grandpa was sitting up straight and looking stern.

'Eavesdropping,' said Grandpa, shaking his head. 'Bad manners, Oliver. If Ma and I are talking together that is a private conversation.'

'I know,' said Oliver miserably. 'The first time I didn't mean to listen but then I began to really, really, really need to know. To know if Pa was coming back . . .'

'We have to trust him,' said Grandpa. 'All of us. You, me, Ma, Titch and Lottie.'

'For how long?' asked Oliver tearfully. 'I have been trusting. But now I'm running out. I can't stretch trust any further. It's like an elastic band that's about to snap. And whenever I ask Ma any questions she just says, *What part of the word "secret" don't you understand?* Why can't *she* trust me?'

Grandpa stirred his chocolate round and round and round as if the answer to all secrets was in there.

'You can hardly want to see your Pa more than I do,' he said. 'You'll have years to spend with your Pa. Next year I'll be ninety. Who knows how long I've got?'

'All the more reason for us to go and find him?' said Oliver eagerly.

'Us?' said Grandpa raising one shaggy white eyebrow and shaking his head. 'Us? You haven't understood me, Oliver.'

'Well, yes!' said Oliver. 'I'm sorry about eavesdropping but I heard you ask Ma for the key to the chest. I heard you say that then we might know *where* he was, even if we didn't know *how* he was. So if we asked her again. Together . . .'

'And do you remember what Ma said?' asked Grandpa. His voice had become stern again.

Oliver hesitated. 'She said she'd promised. Not to open the chest unless there was an emergency,' he said in small voice.

'Would I ask her to break her promise?' asked Grandpa.

'No,' said Oliver in an even smaller voice.

'Would you?' asked Grandpa.

'No,' said Oliver.

'Well then,' said Grandpa. 'And now I think it's time for bed.'

'Yes,' said Oliver. He could feel the tears stinging his eyes. He got off the bed, determined not to cry. 'I'll wash the mugs in the kitchen.'

'Good lad,' said Grandpa.

Oliver took both mugs and the milk pan. He'd just managed to hold all three in one hand while opening the door when Grandpa rose from his chair.

'Oliver?'

Oliver turned to look at him.

'Next time you're in Ma's room you might want to look for a book called *Scottish Folk Stories*. I think you'd find it interesting.'

For all of a minute Oliver stood in the doorway while he took in what Grandpa was saying.

'Yes!' he said. 'Yes, I will! Thank you! Thank you, Grandpa!'

'A pleasure,' said Grandpa. 'Night, night, Oliver. Sleep well.'

But sleeping well was the last thing that Oliver could do. He lay in bed trying to picture the shelves of books in Ma's room, or even the towers on the floor. How many books were there? Had Ma already looked in the chest? Was that why the key had been hung – just for a day maybe – on the hook with the scissors and zips and she simply hadn't got round to putting it back where she kept it?

He fell asleep without any answers. He dreamt of the Grandma he'd seen in the photograph in Grandpa's room. She was making scones at a kitchen table, though it wasn't the kitchen table of *Dizzy Perch* and Big Jim was there. They were drinking tea and talking about steam engines.

In the morning Oliver wondered if he'd been dreaming or if he'd been visited by Grandpa's ghosts.

CHAPTER 8

Detective Work

For the rest of the week Oliver followed Grandpa about until Grandpa got snappy and said he was like an irritating puppy. Oliver felt sure Grandpa knew more than he was prepared to say. Was *Scottish Folk Stories* really a clue? Several times he'd been into Ma's room, surprising her with unexpected cups of tea while trying to look around for the book. It was very difficult trying to look as if you were *not* looking. And anyway, it was impossible. There were shelves labelled History, Biography, Art, Philosophy. But they all seemed to have got jumbled up – history books among art books, books that seemed to have lost their way entirely, not to mention the higgledy-piggledy piles that hadn't yet made it to the shelves. Nowhere could Oliver see a shelf labelled *Stories* and nor did he dare ask, for fear of making Ma suspicious.

Perhaps the book *wasn't* a clue. Perhaps Oliver had imagined it. After all, it had been late at night and with all those ghosts hanging about. Perhaps Grandpa had just been making small talk. But if it *was* a clue, please could it be a slightly bigger, clearer clue. That's what Oliver wanted. But whenever Oliver started on a question, Grandpa acted as if he had no idea what Oliver was talking about.

'About that book . . .' Oliver began.

'What book?' Grandpa said.

'You know, the one you told me to look for . . .'

'Did I? Did I really? Snakes and Ladders. Mad as Hatters!' And Grandpa scratched his head and looked puzzled. 'I'm getting very old and forgetful,' he said, patting Oliver on the back. 'You just do what you have to do.'

Well, what did that mean? Oliver wondered.

All four of them were out on the rocks. It was Grandpa's turn to deliver the week's lesson. It was to be Geology. Or birds. Or Geology *and* birds. Grandpa hadn't quite decided.

Oliver wasn't thinking of either. His head was too full of questions. Was there, he wanted to ask, some kind of message inside *Scottish Folk Stories*? Would he have to read the whole book to find it or was the page marked? Which page? Or maybe a slip of paper inside the book? Was the key to the chest inside the book? And exactly *where* among Ma's many books was this one?

There was no point in asking any of these questions. Grandpa was clearly going to pretend he hadn't said anything at all about *Scottish Folk Stories.* Standing aloft on a high crag, propped up by his stick, his white hair blowing in the wind, an old tartan cape swirling about his shoulders, Grandpa had stopped being the homely, fiddle-playing Grandpa with a room full of memories, photographs and ghosts. He'd become grand. (Grandpa Grand, thought Oliver.) He looked like an old sea captain or a prophet from the bible.

Well, thought Oliver, I'll ask him something else instead.

'I was wondering if Pa's work was something to do with a space mission?' he said, gesturing at the space all round them. 'Or maybe he's calculating how many birds can nest on one cliff?'

For a moment Grandpa looked distinctly alarmed, so that for a crazy minute Oliver thought he might actually be right! Then Grandpa recovered himself.

'This is a Geology lesson, Oliver,' he said. 'Now these rocks . . .' Grandpa switched on his special Teacher voice which was so loud, full throated and important that Oliver wondered if Grandpa imagined he was addressing an audience of fish down below or the birds up above and not just his three grandchildren.

'These rocks,' Grandpa pronounced, 'are

very, very old.'

Titch, perched on a rock and poking about in a gully with a stick to fetch out some shells, looked up. 'How old are you, Grandpa?'

'He's ninety,' said Oliver.

'Very nearly ninety,' Grandpa corrected, 'now, as I was saying . . .'

'So you're as old as these rocks,' persisted Titch. He'd released a very pretty pink and white shell from its crack in the rock.

Grandpa rolled his eyes heavenwards. 'You have no idea,' he told them all, 'of time or age. Some of these rocks were made from the lava of volcanoes, something like four hundred million years ago. FOUR HUNDRED MILLION YEARS AGO!' Grandpa repeated, panicking a flight of seagulls. 'And millions of years ago other rocks – greywackes and siltstones – were laid down at the bottom of the sea four hundred and ten million, four hundred and sixty million years ago!'

Grandpa's voice got louder and louder as he added more millions, waving his arms in the sky as if to take on the whole universe in one lesson.

The numbers made Oliver feel dizzy. Suddenly the time Pa had been away seemed to shrink compared to all these millions of years. Only somehow knowing how old these rocks were didn't help to make him miss Pa any less, or to make the months of waiting any shorter.

'When I'm a million years old, I might very well turn myself into a bird,' said Titch. 'Magically.'

'Silly!' said Lottie. 'For myself, I'd be a mermaid. Every now and again, I'd come out of the sea and sit on a rock and comb my hair.'

'You're both daft!' said Oliver. 'No one's going to live until they're a million.' He was about to add, *or even a hundred*, but didn't want to offend Grandpa.

'Magically!' repeated Lottie as if it was Oliver who was daft if he didn't understand *magically*.

Not that Grandpa appeared to be listening to any of them. Oliver could tell he was off into his Big Summing-up Speech and had all but forgotten his three students.

'And here you can see the work of that great sculptor, the sea!' he announced, gesturing at the cliffs about them. 'Stacks and gullies, cliffs and caves. The sea! The sea! The sea is the master who shapes the world!'

'Magic!' whispered Titch, but nobody heard him.

Really, thought Oliver, beginning to feel cross. Anyone would think it was Grandpa himself who had done all this shaping. And as for being old and forgetful, well, that was obviously rubbish. Old yes. Forgetful, no.

High up as they were, higher up still, Oliver could see a congregation of snowy white gannets. Grandpa had seen them too. Clearly he thought they made a more attentive audience than Oliver, Lottie and Titch.

'Birds of these cliffs,' he began. 'Razorbills, shags, herring gulls, fulmars, puffins and the wonderful gannets.'

The gannets shifted about on their short legs, eyeing the sea with their misty grey eyes, indifferent to Grandpa.

'Their nests are untidy affairs,' said Grandpa, 'made of seaweed and grass, but just watch them fish!'

And as if one of the gannets had heard him, it lifted off from the cliff, folded its wings in tight and plunged head down into the sea as if it was falling from the sky.

'Wow! And wow! And wow!' shouted Grandpa. 'It's going at a hundred miles an hour! Snakes and Ladders! Mad as Hatters! Did you see that? Did you?'

But no one answered. Oliver, Lottie and Titch had decided that Grandpa's lesson was over.

The lesson was over early enough for Oliver to decide, when they got back to *Dizzy Perch*, to make Ma a nice cup of coffee for her elevenses and to try, one more time, to find *Scottish Folk Stories*. Ma didn't seem to hear his knock so he went on in, expecting to find her either sewing or reading. She wasn't doing either which meant she must be out on the balcony. The inner door was closed but Oliver knew that Ma often liked to sit out there when the weather was good.

He put down the coffee and biscuit. This would give him a few minutes to search. Maybe he might just be lucky. He looked round the room half hoping the title would stare out at him or even jump off the shelf, or that he might say *abracadabra* and it would appear.

The coffee was cooling. Ma mustn't catch him nosying about her book shelves. He gave a small rap on the balcony door and took the coffee out to her. He thought he'd find her sitting in her chair, wrapped in shawls and reading. Instead she was leaning over the balcony rail and in that second where he opened the door and she turned to see him he could have sworn she was waving. Then she sank back into her wicker chair.

'Dear Thing!' she said, dropping her arm as if she'd just been patting the frizz of her hair. 'I didn't hear you come in.' She was looking rosier than usual. Or was she blushing?

'Some coffee,' said Oliver, setting the mug down beside her. He sidled round the edge of her chair so that he could look out over the balcony rail. At first he saw nothing. Then he saw a flash of a stripy scarf like a streamer against the sky and heard the faint but unmistakable roar of a motorbike heading out towards Starwater.

'You were waving at someone,' Oliver accused her. 'Do you know him? Who is he?' For he was certain it was the stranger. The man at the bus stop. The man on the beach. The man who seemed to be turning up everywhere.

'I don't know what you're talking about,' said Ma. 'Who on earth would I wave to?'

'I don't know,' said Oliver, miserable and angry, 'maybe someone with a message from Pa? You would tell me, wouldn't you, if you had a message? Or maybe he's too far away to get a message to you?'

'No, no,' said Ma, 'Pa's not out of the country.' She gave him a hug.

'Has he got an office somewhere?' asked

Oliver eagerly, 'or a workshop, like Grandpa?'

'Dear Thing!' said Ma, 'I suppose you could call his laboratory a workshop . . .'

'A laboratory?' Oliver leapt on the word. A laboratory! Scientists and inventors had laboratories. They were rooms where you mixed things together in pots and dishes and hoped to come up with something new. The thought made Oliver grin. Why, a laboratory was like a kitchen!

'Enough!' cried Ma. 'No more questions. *What part of the word "secret"—'*

'Don't you understand,' finished Oliver.

'That's it,' said Ma. 'Now, don't you worry your head about Pa. Do I look anxious? Do I look worried?'

'No,' said Oliver.

'Well then,' said Ma. 'There's no need for you to worry. Try a good book, that's what I always say. Takes your mind off things.'

'Maybe I could look round,' said Oliver. 'Find a book I fancy?' (Like *Scottish Folk Tales*, he was thinking.)

'No need,' said Ma as she trundled back into her bed/book room, 'I'll find you a good story book.' Ma seemed to know exactly where every book was, because in no time at all she'd pulled out a book called *Emil and the Detectives* and handed it to Oliver.

'Dear Thing,' said Ma. 'Let me know when you've finished it and I'll find you something else.'

'Or I could look for myself,' suggested Oliver.

'No need,' said Ma again, 'I'll enjoy choosing for you.'

Oliver went off with *Emil and the Detectives*, feeling much like a detective himself, but a rather lonely one. Well, at least he now had two clues, if you could call them clues. First Grandpa giving him a clue about the key to the chest (and then pretending he hadn't). And now Ma letting slip – he felt sure she hadn't meant to – telling him that Pa was still in the country. At the very least, it was something, he supposed, to know that Pa's laboratory wasn't in America or India or China.

But then as fast as he gathered clues he found more puzzles. He was sure Ma *had* been waving to someone on the beach – and sure too, that it had been the stranger. So why had she lied about it? And why *wasn't* she worried about Pa? That was the most worrying thing of all! She ought to be worried, Oliver thought indignantly. If you loved someone you worried about them, didn't you? Did other wives not care if their husbands didn't come home for months and months and didn't send any messages and went off to do something very secret but didn't tell you what it was?

Maybe Ma herself had a secret. What if she was secretly very fed up waiting for Pa and was about to ride off on the back of the Stranger's motorbike and the three of them would be left with Grandpa who wasn't going to live to be a million, maybe not even a hundred, and then they'd all be stuck at *Dizzy Perch* for ever and ever with no one to look after them.

The thought of all this made Oliver go hot

and cold all over. He lay on his bed and began reading *Emil and the Detectives*. It was all very well for Emil, he thought, when he'd read the first few chapters. Emil found a gang of detectives to help him. Oliver thought about going to find Lottie in her tower or Titch among his stones and pebbles. He knew they both missed Pa but he also knew they weren't worried about him. Not in the way Grandpa was, although he wouldn't or couldn't do anything about it. Not in the way Oliver was. But it didn't feel fair to frighten Lottie and Titch with his own worries.

Oliver put the book down and lay on his back with his head pillowed on his arms. Cezary, he thought. Cezary – his new, his only friend – would understand, maybe even help. Cezary knew what missing someone felt like. Oliver got up and looked out of the window. The tide was far out. He could race along the beach to Starwater.

CHAPTER 9

A Boy From the Clouds

Halfway to Starwater, Oliver was suddenly struck with shyness. What if Cezary and Cheerio weren't on the harbour? What if he had to knock on the door of 3 Seaview Terrace? Had Cezary told his mother about him, Oliver? What if Cezary had found another friend? Why did shyness make your tummy scrunch up and your mouth go dry?

At the harbour all three boats – *Exuberant*, *Magnet* and *Nadzieja* – were roped up against their bollards, bouncing gently in the water as if eager to be off. But the cabin hatch of *Nadzieja* was firmly closed and there was no one in sight. No fishermen. No Cheerio, no Cezary.

The only sign of life was a yellow helicopter that circled the harbour and then flew off in the distance.

Oliver headed for the Post Office Stores because that's what he always did when he came to Starwater. And once there, he did what he always did and Mrs Tansley waited for him to do it.

'Good morning, Mrs Tansley,' he said. 'Any letters for Coggin?'

'Good morning, Oliver Coggin,' said Mrs Tansley as she ducked under the Stores part of the counter and came up on the Post Office side in her postmaster's hat. She gave a brief glance at the pigeon hole marked C. 'Nothing today,' she said as she always said. 'Maybe tomorrow.' And Oliver nodded, as if he really believed her.

He was about to turn away when he felt a hand on his shoulder.

'Tomorrow is good,' said a voice. Oliver turned to find Cezary's father. 'I am here with savings for tomorrow,' he said to Mrs Tansley. 'Bring more family here.'

'How many more?' asked Mrs Tansley taking the two pound coins pushed across the counter.

'Three,' said Cezary's father. 'Two boys and a girl. We are missing.'

'Them,' said Mrs Tansley finishing his sentence.

'Them,' said Cezary's father and, turning to Oliver, 'And Cezary is missing a friend. You come to see him? I invite!'

'Thank you, yes,' said Oliver, thinking, though he didn't say, that he'd been about to invite himself.

They walked up to Seaview Terrace together. Cezary and Cheerio came running down the street to meet them, Cheerio as bouncy as the boats in the harbour, his tail flip-flapping Oliver's bare legs.

'I wonder when you next come,' said Cezary.

Compared to *Dizzy Perch*, 3 Seaview Terrace was like a doll's house. Inside, a tiny hall led to a narrow kitchen on one side and a small square sitting room on the other. There didn't appear to be a bathroom. Oliver wondered how, if and when Cezary's two brothers and one sister arrived, they would all have room to eat and sleep. One thing was certain – no one would ever feel lonely in 3 Seaview Terrace.

Cezary's mother seemed just the right size for the house being small, neat and shiny. She wore her hair in plaits on top of her head and her smile was like Cezary's. 'Cezary hope you come,' she said, shaking Oliver's hand as if she too had been hoping he would come.

'Best if we sit outside,' said Cezary. There was a small blue bench at the front of the house. It looked down first on the garden (the family were obviously growing vegetables, for Oliver could see leafy tops of sprouting lettuce) and then over the rocks to the sea. Cezary brought out two glasses of apple juice and a plate of biscuits. Cheerio lay across their feet. The yellow helicopter was back. It did two more circuits of the harbour. Oliver shaded his eyes to look up at it.

'What's that helicopter doing?' he asked. 'I haven't seen it around here before.'

'It comes and goes,' said Cezary. 'It comes out of the clouds, like you. You boy from the clouds! We think it looking for someone. Maybe police.'

Although it was quite a sunny day, Oliver shivered a little. It felt odd being called a boy from the clouds, as if somehow he wasn't quite real.

'You tell me about your how do you say? Your Perch,' said Cezary. 'Is castle? And someone missing? You say you understand missing.'

Well, now was his chance, thought Oliver. In Cezary's warm brown eyes he could see nothing but friendship. The apple juice was sweet, Cheerio warm on his feet, but suddenly he was stuck for words. How could he possibly explain *Dizzy Perch*? Its place high up on the cliffs, its funicular railway, Lottie's tower, the two balconies. And where to start on his family? How Ma never left the house. How Grandpa knew ghosts. How it was Pa who was missing.

'Your brothers and your sister,' he began. 'Do you know where they are?'

''Course I know where they are!' said Cezary. 'With my grandparents in Gdansk. They look after them until we send money to come here.'

'Pa,' said Oliver, and the very word seemed to stick in his throat. 'He's the missing one, but I don't know where he is.'

'You don't know where? You have him lost?' asked Cezary, astonished.

'He has work,' said Oliver. *(What don't you understand about the word 'secret'?)*

'Ah!' said Cezary. 'He earning money for family. Then comes home.'

Oliver concentrated on the apple juice. Then, 'Yes,' he said. 'That's what he's doing. He'll be home soon.' He got a lump in his throat when he said it and, as if he understood, Cezary punched his arm and said, 'Yes, and my brothers and sister.'

'Tell me,' said Cezary. 'Up in the clouds, d'you all wear these bright colours so you can see each other?'

Oliver looked down at himself. He'd forgotten he was back in his silk red, yellow and blue striped shorts. 'Oh all the time!' he laughed. 'We cloud people.'

'I come and see you in your perch?' said Cezary.

'One day,' said Oliver. When Pa is safely home, he was thinking and on impulse he gave Cezary a hug.

Cezary watched him go – back along the Creel Road and then over the rocks this time because the tide was coming in.

'I think he lost his father,' he said to his own father.

All the way back to *Dizzy Perch*, Oliver wished he'd found some way of telling Cezary how worried he was without telling him that Pa's work was secret, possibly dangerous. Could you tell half the truth about something? Was half the truth true enough? He walked slowly, the whole truth seemed almost too heavy to carry on his own.

He was late home. Lottie and Titch were hanging hopefully about the kitchen. Even Ma had appeared, wondering what was for supper. 'Something quick and easy,' said Grandpa, 'because it's music night.'

About once a month Grandpa declared it was music night and they all groaned and complained and then they all enjoyed it.

'Dance, I've heard say,' said Grandpa, directing his remarks at Titch and Lottie, 'is as important as arithmetic.'

Easy for those two, thought Oliver. Titch was a tap-dancer. Grandpa had fixed metal taps on his shoes and Titch practised everywhere from the spiral staircase to the rocks outside. When Titch went down in the bucket seat of the funicular railway, you could see his feet tapping in the air. Practising. 'Dear Thing,' said Ma. 'If you're not careful you'll forget how to walk.'

For Lottie, dancing meant dressing up. 'Tonight I'm flamenco,' she said, when they'd all gathered in the sitting room and Ma had moved the rug so that Titch could tap over the whole floor.

Grandpa tuned up his fiddle. Oliver slouched

in one of the two sofas.

Lottie was first. Ma had made her a flamenco dress out of a mixture of old red and purple curtains. She'd made lots of frills and flounces. Grandpa had made castanets. Lottie flounced round the room, snappping her castanets and occasionally stamping her feet and tossing her hair as if she was angry. Everyone laughed and clapped.

Ma was next. Ma read a poem called 'A Red, Red Rose'. It was a very sad poem and Ma half spoke and half sang it. Oliver only began to listen when Ma got to the last two verses:

> *Till a' the seas gang dry, my Dear*
> *And the rocks melt wi' the sun:*
> *I will love thee still, my Dear,*
> *While the sands o' life shall run.*

> *And fare thee weel, my only Luve!*
> *And fare thee weel, a while!*
> *And I will come again, my Luve,*
> *Tho' it were ten thousand mile!*

Ma had to dry her eyes when she finished it. Why, thought Oliver, feeling the tears prick his own eyes, Ma was really missing Pa much more than she would tell any of them. Probably he was her true Dear Thing. He wished the song was more hopeful. If they had to wait until the rocks melted with the sun for Pa to come home, it would be a very, very long wait. And what if he were *ten thousand miles* away? No, Ma had said he wasn't out of the country.

Grandpa had come to sit next to him on the sofa. He nudged Oliver in the ribs. 'Maybe time to get us all a drink,' he said.

'No one's asked for one,' protested Oliver.

'But I think they'd like one,' Grandpa persisted, giving Oliver two nudges this time.

'Three down, four across,' he hissed in Oliver's ear.

'What?' asked Oliver. It sounded like a clue for a crossword puzzle.

Grandpa had stood up and begun tuning his fiddle again, for Titch this time.

'You can read us something later,' he said to

Oliver, nudging him up and out of the sofa and whispering again, 'three down, four across.'

And suddenly Oliver got it. *Three down, four across*! Grandpa was telling him where to find *Scottish Folk Stories*.

Ma was out of her room. Titch was dancing to Grandpa's fiddle.

Oliver took the stairs two at a time.

Ma's room, without Ma in it, was curiously spooky, as if all the people inside the books were living there too, breathing behind the covers, listening to him.

'Three down, four across!' Oliver repeated. Three shelves down, fourth book across, but which of the three walls?

And of course it was the third wall he looked at. Even then he almost missed it. He'd expected *Scottish Folk Stories* to be a fat, important looking book. It was thin and old, the title on the spine so faded he could hardly read it and it was jammed in between *Aesop's Fables*, *Chambers Dictionary* and *Grimm's Fairy Tales*.

Very carefully Oliver eased it out. Inside it

was entirely empty. Not so much a book as a box, and in the box, small and innocent, a key.

'Thank you, Grandpa!' Oliver said to all the listening books. 'Thank you, thank you!' And, pocketing the key, he slid the book back into its place and ran downstairs, almost forgetting to stop at the kitchen and fetch a jug of water that probably nobody wanted.

Titch was still in mid-tap when he went back into the sitting room and set the jug and five glasses on the table.

Grandpa looked up from his fiddle, raising his eyebrows in a question.

Oliver nodded.

Grandpa winked.

'What are you going to read for us, Dear Thing?' Ma asked him.

'I think I'll read a bit of *Emil and the Detectives*,' said Oliver and could hardly stop grinning. Who needed a gang of detectives? Not him!

Chapter 10

How Much Missing Can a Person Put Up With?

The very next morning Oliver was ready to act. With the key in his pocket he could hardly wait until breakfast was over. This was it! This was his moment! He could slide into Pa's room while everyone else was out of the way, close the door behind him, open the chest and – FIND OUT! Oliver the Detective was on the job! He had his hand on the door knob of Pa's room when Ma appeared.

Ma not reading. Ma, clearly in a flap because all her clothes flapped about her. Oliver wondered if something had happened to Ma overnight or if he hadn't really looked at her lately because now she was looking thin and pale. Worry had pulled her face out of shape, made her frizz frizzier.

'Titch,' said Ma.

Oliver snatched his hand off the door knob as if it was hot and buried the key to the chest deep in his pocket.

'What about him?' he asked.

'Missing,' said Ma. 'When did you last see him?'

'He didn't come for breakfast,' said Oliver, 'so it would be yesterday. He was hanging about while I was trying to cook – getting in the way.'

Ma sighed. 'So what did you do?' she asked.

'I told him to scoot,' said Oliver.

Ma sighed again only it was a longer, heavier sigh. 'Lottie told him to scram. Grandpa told him to hop it. I told him to buzz off.'

Oliver was alarmed to find that Ma was crying.

'And now he has,' she said. 'The Dear Thing has scooted, hopped it and buzzed off. Run away,' she said, dabbing her eyes with the edge of her shawl. 'He's done what we told him to do – scooted, hopped it . . .'

Oliver interrupted her before she could repeat it all again. 'You just go back to your room and I'll bring you a hot chocolate,' he said soothingly. 'Remember what you told me? A book can take your mind off things.'

'Maybe not everything,' said Ma, sniffing.

'Titch can't have gone far,' said Oliver. He was feeling nicely important. 'Lottie and I will find him.'

Titch hadn't gone far. He hadn't scooted or buzzed off; he had simply taken the huff and gone into hiding. He'd got the idea from Biggles. For three days in February, Biggles had gone missing.

On Monday, Tuesday, Wednesday they had looked for him everywhere. A gloom like a dark cloud had settled on all of them. Oliver had said he couldn't get to sleep without Biggles at the bottom of his bed. Ma had said her lap felt odd without Biggles snuggling in. Grandpa had played a lament that made them all feel worse. Lottie put on a black dress and said she was going gothic.

And then on the fourth day, Thursday, Biggles had strolled back in without so much as a by-your-leave. He'd looked a bit skinny and his ginger fur was decidedly ruffled and one of his white ears had a nip taken out of it, but it was Biggles himself. Their Biggles and they were all delighted to see him.

Oliver had made him a special fish supper. Ma took him on her lap and brushed him until Biggles's eyes turned into slits of pleasure. And everyone had stroked and fussed over him and offered him cat-treats and cuddles.

It would be very nice, thought Titch, to be fussed over and cuddled and given treats. But people had to miss you first. Oliver had got lots of big hugs when he was late home from Starwater and they'd thought he wasn't coming home. And Pa would probably be given an ENORMOUS treat and lots and lots and lots of hugs when he came home. Going missing,

Titch reasoned, was the thing to do. He took his Ted, two apples, three biscuits, a carton of orange juice and put them all in a knapsack, then he rode down on the funicular railway to the beach and found a nice handy cave and waited to be found.

Only it was rather a long time before anyone missed him. At least it seemed a long time to Titch, although in truth it was only a morning and half of an afternoon. Long enough for Titch to have eaten the apples and biscuits and finished the carton of orange juice. The May sunshine was pale. A shower was drifting in across the sea. Inside the cave it was not too warm. Titch hadn't thought to bring a jersey or a blanket. He wished he could go out onto the beach and sit in the little sunshine there was.

'But we can't do that,' he told Ted, 'because we're hiding.' He snuggled Ted into his tummy. 'But don't worry,' he continued, 'when they find us we'll get lots of treats. Olly will make us a special cake and Lottie will try and kiss us and

119

Ma will say she's very, very sorry for telling me to buzz off.'

Up in the house, Oliver and Lottie began searching for him – Lottie under protest.

'He's a pest,' she grumbled. 'He'll just turn up. In fact I'm not sure I care if he doesn't!'

'He's your little brother,' said Oliver. 'I think you care more for Biggles!'

'Oh well,' said Lottie, but she grinned and looked guilty. 'What d'you bet we don't find him and he just jumps out at us. Ta-dah!'

For the briefest of moments Oliver wondered what it would be like if they *didn't* find Titch. There was a sudden hollow feeling in his chest, as though a part of him – a Titch part – had gone missing. How much missing could a person put up with? he asked himself. First Pa and now Titch.

'Of course we'll find him,' he said with more confidence than he felt.

It was late afternoon before they decided that Titch was nowhere in the house. Lottie had stopped joking. She'd tied her hair up as if this might help her to search. Her face looked pinched, her freckles pale.

They had looked in Titch's bedroom. The room felt sad without him – his collections laid out on the floor, woolly toys on his bed, but no Ted. Oliver looked in the clothes cupboard. All Titch's jeans and jerseys were still there.

'If he's run away he can't have gone far,' Oliver said.

The weather, which had begun the day cheerfully, had turned dark and gusty. The showers of early morning had grown wilder. The gannets flung themselves about in the wind, yapping to each other and heading for their inlets in the cliffs.

'I hope he's not on the cliff path,' said Lottie. 'He hasn't got a cagoul.' She sounded quite motherly.

'Or a jersey,' said Oliver, 'but at least he knows his way about on the cliffs. Ma says he's like a little goat.'

Even so, neither of them liked to think of

121

Titch out there on the cliffs feeling unwanted.

'I didn't really want him to scram,' said Lottie

'Or scoot,' said Oliver. He felt bad remembering how tearful Titch had been when he'd sent him away. 'We'd better look on the beach.'

Oliver found them each an anorak. He packed a bag with one of Titch's jerseys, warm socks, a rug. Then he added bananas, three slices of fruit cake, a packet of crisps, a bottle of water.

They rode down on the funicular railway, holding hands.

The sky had darkened as if a storm was coming. In both directions the beach was empty. Empty and lonely. The cliffs, looming above them, seemed dark and knowing, capable of hiding a small boy and not telling. Seagulls squalled out to sea as if they'd heard some very bad news. The wind blew sand in their faces. Rain dashed inland. Oliver and Lottie could hardly hear each other speak.

Oliver cupped his hands round his mouth and shouted.

'Titch! Tiiiiiiiitch! TITCH!'

But if Titch heard him, he didn't reply.

When the wind got up and the rain became more than a shower, Titch moved far back inside the cave, cold and frightened. He wondered what time it was? Even what day it was? Now and again he tried to comfort himself with the words of the hide-and-seek game. 'Coming ready or not,' he told Ted. In the game someone always finds you, thought Titch. But they didn't take so long about it. Had anyone ever died, forgotten in a cave? Try as he might, Titch couldn't help a small sob or two.

'We'll search the caves,' said Oliver.

They divided the beach between them. Lottie searched the smaller caves because she could squeeze into them. Some were so shallow not even a boy as little as Titch could hide inside. Others, scarily, went so far back into the cliffs that you felt you were going back in time too. Oliver kicked himself for not bringing a torch.

It was the faint sob that did it. A familiar little sob. An unmistakable Titch-in-trouble kind of sob that Oliver had known since Titch was a baby when the sob had been more of a wah-wah-wah noise.

'Titch!' he shouted. 'Titch!' calling down the mouth of the cave.

A hiccup. Another sob. And, 'I'm here, Olly! I'm here!'

And out crawled Titch, tear-stained, his hair covered in cobwebs, a rather soggy Ted tucked under one arm.

To Oliver's surprise he found relief turning to anger.

'What on earth did you think you were doing?' he shouted, taking Titch up in a huge hug. 'Don't you ever do anything so daft again.' And, setting Titch down on the beach, 'Here, have a banana. Have two. Have some water.'

Despite the wind and the rain, the three of them had a kind of picnic on the beach, sitting on some rocks with Titch wrapped in the rug and eating most of the food, Lottie's hair coming undone and flying in the wind like a ragged flag. Then all three rode up to *Dizzy Perch* on the funicular, Titch sitting on Oliver's knees.

Oliver held Titch tight. He was struggling with a mix of relief and impatience. Why oh why had Titch chosen the very day – the very morning – when the key to the chest was in his hand, to play such an awful hide-and-seek game?

'You are never to scoot, scram, hop it or buzz off ever again,' Ma told Titch when he was delivered to her, safe, sound, tired and dirty.

Everyone made such a fuss of him that Titch almost thought that going missing had been worth it. Almost. Until he remembered the cold of the cave and how dark it had seemed and then he gave a kind of shiver and thought that going missing might be all right for cats like Biggles who knew how to find their way home again but it wasn't all right for him.

It was dusk. The rain had cleared, the sky changed its colours, as if trying out a new palette. Oliver fingered the key to the chest to make sure it was still safe in his pocket. How long would he have to wait? Missing Titch made it seem even more urgent that he should find Pa. What if they *hadn't* found Titch? What if Titch had died down there in the cold cave? You shouldn't leave a missing person for too long, Oliver told himself. Not a little brother. Not a Pa. Desperation made him tense all over. He *must* open the chest. And soon. Certainly before Ma had time to check if the key was still inside *Scottish Folk Stories*. Would he have time after supper? If not then, he'd have to wait until Ma had stopped her midnight wanderings and gone to sleep. It was unbearable! Did Emil have so many difficulties to overcome?

After supper Lottie actually helped with the washing up. Oliver saw Ma and Grandpa going off into the sitting room together. Something about the look on their faces and the way they were nodding at each other made the thought leap into Oliver's mind that there might be news. Grandpa had been down to Starwater. Had there, just this once, been a message at the Post Office Stores? A message from Pa? A message to say he was in trouble? Or, perish the thought, a message from kidnappers?

Avoiding the floorboard creaks, Oliver knelt and listened at the door.

'No word, I suppose,' said Grandpa.

'Need you ask,' said Ma. 'No word and no money.'

Oliver was startled. Whenever he went shopping in Starwater, Ma gave him money from the saucepan where she kept it. He'd never given much thought to how it was that there was always enough. The pot seemed to fill itself which, now that he thought about it, was plainly ridiculous.

'We can't go on much longer like this,' said Grandpa. 'You should do something . . .'

A heavy sigh from Ma. 'I promised,' she reminded him, 'not to disturb him unless there was an emergency.'

'Running out of money *is* close to an emergency in my opinion,' said Grandpa. 'And do you think there's a chance that that son of mine is going to come home before I die?'

'You're not going to die,' said Ma firmly, as if that was an order. 'You're fit as a fiddle.'

'I'm eighty-nine,' said Grandpa. 'You never know. And you don't look that grand yourself.'

'I'm fine,' said Ma.

'Lovelorn, that's how you look,' said Grandpa. 'Pining.'

(Was that a tearful sniff from Ma?) 'Trust him,' said Ma. 'I'm sure he'll send a message soon.'

'If he doesn't, we're in trouble,' said Grandpa.

Oliver's feet had got cramp. He rubbed them until they worked again then crept up to his room. Here was something else to try and work out. This wasn't *Pa* in trouble, this was Pa leaving all of *them* in trouble – Ma, Grandpa, Lottie and Titch. Didn't Pa care about Ma? Had he forgotten to send money? What if they starved? Had he forgotten all of them? It was a terrible, terrible thought.

It seemed to take ages for everyone in *Dizzy Perch* to go to sleep. Ma's light stayed on, which meant she was still reading. Grandpa, obviously too worried to sleep, was playing his fiddle, repeating the same tune over and over again. Titch was coughing. Up in her tower Lottie was singing. Eventually the fiddle stopped and Grandpa's snores travelled up through the house.

Oliver had a hard time *not* falling asleep. He kept his window wide open so he didn't get too snug and every now and again he tiptoed into the bathroom and splashed his face with cold water.

It was midnight before, apart from Grandpa's snores and Titch's coughs, the house was quiet. In his bare feet Oliver crept down the stairs, past Titch's room (more coughs), past Ma's room, past Grandpa's, then he was there, opening the door of Pa's study – surely it didn't usually creak like this? – shutting it behind him. Panic had made him breathless. He had to stop and take several deep breaths.

The room itself seemed different at night. Moonlight seemed to occupy it like a lodger or a squatter who had come to take over. Perhaps this was what happened to unoccupied rooms, thought Oliver. The moon or nature or . . . no, he wasn't going to think about ghosts, not even one of Grandpa's . . . took over. He switched on the small standard lamp by the bed. It didn't help, only added an ill-looking yellow light to the room. And there was a smell. The stale smell of a room rarely aired, a room not lived in.

Get a grip, Oliver told himself and kneeling down in front of the chest he put the key in the lock and turned it.

CHAPTER 11

Berkellium, Actinium, Dysprosium, Tellurium

The key turned easily, as if the chest had been waiting for someone – anyone, Oliver – to open it. It was an old chest, more like a sailor's trunk. The corners were bound in metal. The lid was studded and heavy. Oliver eased it back. He was so nervous that it wouldn't have surprised him if something had jumped out at him. He discovered he'd been holding his breath but now he breathed normally.

There was nothing in the chest to scare him. In fact there was nothing in the chest that seemed even remotely interesting! He was faced with a mound of old clothes, a couple of rugs, a flurry of cross moths and a squashed hat that might once have been rather handsome. Oliver put it on. Then he found an old jersey and put that on over his pyjama jacket. It was somehow comforting to be wearing Pa's clothes. Not as good as finding him, of course, but as if he was closer. Oliver hugged the jersey about him. The arms were too long and it came down to his knees. He punched the hat into the shape it would have had when Pa wore it, which was a kind of trilby.

And then, because he didn't know what else to do and because worrying and borrowing/ stealing the key and staying awake had all been so difficult, he began taking everything out of the chest and giving it a good shake. Another flurry of shocked moths flew about his head. Oliver flapped them away. He didn't know whether to laugh or cry, he felt so disappointed. All this bother for a chest of old clothes!

He threw a couple of rugs on the bed, wound a faded tartan scarf round his neck, made a pile of patched jeans and much-washed shirts and was just about to give up and stuff everything back when he felt something hard. In fact all along the bottom of the chest, as neatly packed as bricks in a wall, was a layer of notebooks, each stiffly backed in cardboard, each labelled *Discovery* with a date and, in red ink, the words *Top Secret*.

Oliver sat back on his heels. Which book to look at? He picked one at random. It was full of sums, numbers mixed up with letters of the alphabet and diagrams that made no sense whichever way Oliver looked at them. If this was a Discovery, what on earth was it of? He tried a second notebook. This one seemed to contain a recipe, but a recipe for what? And of what? Oliver had never heard of the ingredients: *berkellium, actinium, dysprosium, tellurium* . . . What was it with all these 'ium' words? Would Grandpa understand them? Were they a sort of code?

He was just about to give up, shut the lid, lock the chest, go to bed, when he realised that the notebooks were laid in such a way as to form yet another kind of lid and that hidden under this lid were coils of rope, a First Aid kit, a Swiss Army knife, a Gotcha Rescue Kit and at the very bottom, a clipboard. The Rescue Kit gave him goosebumps. What if he had to rescue Pa? He drew out the clipboard. Attached was a map, a calendar and a page of handwriting.

Oliver unclipped the map, spread it out on the floor and moved the lamp so he could examine it clearly. It was a map of Scotland. It suddenly occurred to Oliver that a map, any map, told a story if you knew how to read it and that this map was telling him something very important about Pa. Someone – Pa? – had drawn a wriggly line all along the coast almost to the top of the map and then across (turning left was how Oliver saw it) and stopping at a dot with a ring round it. In tiny writing there was a name beside the dot. Oliver held it under the lamp. *Auchterlaldy*, he read. *Auchterlaldy*. Was that where Pa was?

He folded the map up very carefully and looked at the calendar. It showed two years and various dates were ringed on it in red and green ink. At the bottom, against a red ring was the word *home* and against a green ring the word *away.*

Was this Pa's plan? Oliver looked for red rings. There was one round February 2nd. Had Pa meant to be home then? Why, it was the end of May – heading for June! Surely Ma and Grandpa knew about these dates, knew that Pa should have been home? Sometimes grown-ups were reasonable and patient to the point of absolute foolishness, thought Oliver. He sat on the floor and counted the days on the calendar. There were eighty-seven days between February 2nd and today's date of Wednesday, May 28th. Eighty-seven! Almost four months! Why, anything could have happened to Pa in four months, eighty-seven days. Anything! With a rising panic Oliver turned to the last page of the clipboard. The handwriting sprawled in a spidery way over a page of sea-blue paper.

Dear Joe, he read. (Who on earth was Joe?)

This is a copy of the letter which you already possess. I put it here for safe-keeping – well, in case something should happen to you that would prevent you acting on my behalf.

    As you know, some of my experiments are top secret. When it comes to medicines or new biological knowledge it's a sad fact that there is always someone, or rather ~~someones~~ *ready to steal the results of my research and then apply what should be a remedy for good, to an evil purpose. Science, alas, can often work in two ways.*

    This, as you know, is why I need to keep my laboratory far away and in a secret place. It's the safest way. For the same reason I bought Dizzy Perch thinking it was the safest place for my dear Maisie, Oliver, Lottie and Terence. I'm for ever in your debt for agreeing to keep an eye on them in my absence. I suspect that Oliver, my eldest boy, has inherited my kind of imaginative curiosity. Keep a particular eye on him, please Joe.

(In the semi-darkness of the study Oliver blushed. He re-read the words again – *'my eldest boy has inherited my kind of imaginative curiosity'* – just thinking he was like his Pa made him feel taller, stronger. He carried on reading.)

It is almost impossible for me to know how long my current work will be, but I hope to be back with you no later than February 2nd. You may need to be patient – they will all need to be patient!

Should there be an emergency, you must speak to Maisie who will have the key to the chest that is inside my study. I have Maisie's promise that, for the safety of the children, she will not look until she has word from me – and that word will come from you, Joe.

Inside the chest you will find a map that will enable you to locate me. Act swiftly.

In addition, I'm aware that the cliffs around Dizzy Perch can be very dangerous. So I thought it wise to leave you everything you might need in the way of a rescue kit. I do hope Grandpa keeps the funicular railway well oiled. Once a week should do it.

(Oh, thought Oliver, all this rescue stuff was for them, not Pa!)

Look after my little ones for me. I know I am not the best father. I am often so absorbed in my work I forget everything. Meals. Sleep. Family. But at heart I love them all dearly. And you too, Joe – friend of my childhood, you've been as a brother to me and I thank you from the bottom of my heart.

Amos.

Oliver folded the map very small and put it in his pocket. He kept Pa's jersey, hat and scarf but everything else, including the letter, he put back in the chest, shut the lid and locked it.

How long had he been in Pa's study? The sky was just beginning to lighten, the birds beginning to wake up. He didn't know what to think or feel. Part of him felt proud to think of his Pa doing important work. The letter spoke of *new biological knowledge.* What if it was something that might help the planet? Or look after animals that would otherwise die? Pa might win a great prize? Or – and this was the part that made him feel scared – whatever the discovery was, those *someones* Pa wrote about, the someones who wanted to use Pa's research for – what was it *evil purpose*? – might have succeeded. Might have captured Pa and stolen his research.

I hope to be back with you no later than February 2nd, Pa had written. He was months late! And who was Joe? Whoever he was, childhood friend, sort-of brother, had Pa sent him word?

Oliver crept out of the study. He needed to think it all through. He needed to sleep. He was half-way up the stairs when he heard Titch (only Pa called him Terence) coughing. Oliver hesitated. Should he call Ma? But then she'd wonder why he was up and about and dressed in Pa's jersey and hat.

Then he thought of how cold Titch had been when he and Lottie had found him in the cave. Cold and shivery. He crept quietly into Titch's room. In the dawn light Titch's bedclothes looked as if a fight had been going on with pillows every which way and Ted thrown on the floor. In between coughs, Titch was tossing and turning as if his bed was full of needles. Oliver picked up Ted and pulled the duvet back over him, but Titch flung it off again. Oliver felt his forehead. It was burning hot.

'Titch, Titch,' he whispered. 'I'm going to get you some water and something for your cough. Titch? Titch?'

Titch rolled over, opened his eyes and stared up at Oliver.

'Pa!' he said and held up his arms.

It was dawn before Titch's fever had cooled and his cough had eased.

'I thought you were Pa,' Titch said wistfully.

'I know,' said Oliver. 'I miss him too. A lot.'

'A lot,' Titch echoed. 'But you're here, big bruv.'

'You've had a fever, little bruv,' Oliver told him snuggling him down. He'd taken off Pa's hat and jersey. And he'd made a decision.

Or rather he'd woken up after a brief two hours sleep with the decision made. (What was it Grandpa often said about decisions? That they often come to you when you're asleep because that's when your mind works freely.) Well, Grandpa was right. But Oliver didn't plan to tell him about this decision. During breakfast, while Ma was out of her room, he'd managed to slip the chest key back inside *Scottish Folk Stories*.

Enough's enough, Oliver's mind said to him when he woke up. *Enough's enough*. Just that. Clear as anything. Certain, sure. *Ma is lovelorn, Titch is poorly, we're running out of money and Pa is almost four months late. Why wait for the mysterious Joe? It was time to go and find Pa.*

CHAPTER 12

The Finding Way

And for the first few hours of dawn as the sky slowly lightened, Oliver felt very brave. The map, with its red and green circles, was burning a hole in his pocket. Whenever he could, he took it out to look at it again and run his finger up the wiggly pencil line. Auchterlaldy seemed a long way away. How to get there? How to get away without anyone knowing?

Since coming to *Dizzy Perch*, Oliver had never been further than Starwater. Probably it was part of Pa's notion of keeping them safe. Oliver could almost imagine Pa saying to himself *a nice big house and a beach to play on – what more could children want?* Well, thought Oliver now, talking back to an imaginary Pa, possibly quite a lot more. After all, wasn't there a world out there? Oliver felt quite dizzy just thinking of the size of it. America! Italy! Russia! Poland!

Cezary! Cezary was twelve. Cezary had travelled. He'd travelled all the way from Poland to Starwater. He'd know how to get to Auchterlaldy. He might (and Oliver felt a sudden surge of hope) even come with him.

The tide was out. Oliver whizzed down on the funicular and ran along the beach until he was out of breath and had to slow down. At 3 Seaview Terrace Cezary was helping his mother with the washing. The garden looked down over the sea. The washing – thin T-shirts, dungarees, a faded dress and some shorts – danced on the line as if eager to escape from their pegs and blow away.

'You would like a drink?' Cezary's mother offered at once. 'You've been running.'

'No thanks,' said Oliver, 'I just need to talk to Cezary.'

'Ah Cezary likes talking to you,' said Mrs

Bajek. 'You nearly brother.' And she smiled a little sadly. 'Cez, you take Oliver for walk. Walk and talk, yes?' (Cheerio pricked up his ears.)

The boys walked down to the harbour and sat on the wall, Cheerio prancing ahead of them. Cezary sat and listened and nodded as all Oliver's worries tumbled out of him. How Pa should have been home and wasn't. How Ma was pining. How Grandpa was old and didn't want to die before his son came home. How they were running short of money. How Titch was poorly. How they were all – how he, Oliver missed his Pa like – like . . .

'Like hole in heart,' Cezary finished for him. Cheerio whined as if sensing sadness.

'Yes,' said Oliver, swallowing a lump in his throat. He brought the map out of his pocket. Was it safe to show Cezary? Something in his heart said that it was. He thought of Pa's Joe, a childhood friend. Now Cezary was his.

'This is very secret,' he said.

'You trust me,' said Cezary.

Oliver spread the map out on the wall.

Cezary turned it this way and that to follow the wriggly line Pa had drawn.

'Ah!' he said. 'This is good journey. You go by the Loch Ness Monster.'

'What?' Oliver's heart sank. This morning's decision suddenly seemed a very bad one.

'On the bus,' said Cezary. 'I can't go bussing because we are saving all money, but I like looking at the journeys. We have book of pictures of England and Scotland. We like to take pretend journeys.'

'About this monster . . .' said Oliver in a small voice.

Cezary laughed. 'I think only story . . . who knows? But I think a big, big loch. You are going to the Scottish Highlands. You are lucky boy.'

'You know more about Scotland than I do,' said Oliver. (In Oliver's head the world was growing larger by the minute.) 'Anyway,' he continued, 'I don't feel very lucky. D'you think you might come with me?'

Cezary gave Oliver's arm a friendly punch. 'I think this is *your* adventure,' he said. 'Some things you need to do alone. Anyway, there's the bus fare . . .'

'The bus fare . . .' echoed Oliver dismally. Why hadn't he thought he would need money?

Cezary jumped down from the wall. 'Come on,' he said, 'we'll find the times of the bus and how much you pay.' Cheerio ran ahead as if glad of some movement at last.

They headed for the Post Office Stores. How strange it was, Oliver thought, that it wasn't just a bus taking him to find his Pa, but some kind of unstoppable decision he seemed to have made in his sleep and now, however scared he was, there was no going back on it.

Mrs Tansley slipped her specs up on her head and searched through a box of timetables. Eventually she slid her specs back on her nose and pushed 'Bus X254' through the grille at them. 'Twice a week. Tuesdays and Thursdays going,' she said, 'change at Loch Wardle.'

'Then what?' asked Oliver.

'Then, Oliver Coggin, it looks as if you walk,' said Mrs Tansley, laughing as if this was the best joke she'd heard all morning. The specs went up on her head again. 'Return Wednesdays and Fridays,' she said. 'You going on your own?' Her eyes, grey and curious, peered at Oliver doubtfully.

For about five seconds Oliver hesitated. Then the words of Pa's letter came back to him – *I suspect that my eldest boy has inherited my kind of imaginative curiosity*. Then 'Yes,' he said firmly. 'Yes I am going on my own.'

Cezary was grinning at him. 'Tomorrow's Thursday,' he said.

Oliver grinned back. 'Yes!' he said.

'Fare's sixteen pound fifty,' said Mrs Tansley. 'Bus leaves at five a.m. You pay the driver. And no, there isn't any post for Coggin.' She took off her Post Office hat, disappeared under the counter and re-appeared in the Stores half of the shop.

Sixteen pounds fifty! Oliver echoed. How was he to get that amount? The only way would be to take the shopping money from Ma's saucepan. If there was enough, that is.

'I don't know how I can get to Starwater for five a.m.,' he said to Cezary. 'The tide will be in and it will still be dark. The cliff path will be very difficult.'

'I have the answer,' said Cezary. 'You sleep in our boat tonight.'

'In *Nadzieja*?' Oliver's effort to pronounce the boat made Cezary laugh.

'In English I think it means *Hope*,' he said. 'A good name for us. A good name for you.' Cheerio wagged an agreement.

'Yes,' said Oliver, 'and thank you. But what if your father wants to go out fishing early in the morning?' His heart seemed to be beating at twice its usual speed.

'You will be off boat by then,' said Cezary, 'and on your finding way.'

There was so much to do that Oliver hardly had time to feel nervous. Back at *Dizzy Perch* he packed what he thought he would need for the journey. A packet of jam sandwiches, two apples, a banana and a bottle of water. Then spare socks (though he couldn't quite think why), his oldest and favourite jersey, his trainers, a big hankie of Grandpa's, Pa's hat from the chest, an alarm clock. He hid everything under his bed.

His plan was to slip away after supper. During supper would be the only time when Ma was out of her room. If he was quick, he could slip in and take – borrow, for somehow or other he'd return it – the shopping money from the saucepan. Last time Ma had given him shopping money, he'd seen (at least) two ten-pound notes. Fingers crossed they were still there. If there wasn't enough money well, he'd just have to try and stow away on the bus! Would that be possible? He hadn't a clue.

He spent the afternoon cooking. It was the least he could do to leave enough food for everyone. He did a big bake – bread, a pie, jam tarts – no one would starve. As usual cooking calmed him. He wondered if Pa liked his laboratory as much as he, Oliver, liked his kitchen.

Supper seemed to last for ever! Between cottage pie and baked apples, he sneaked into Ma's room. The money saucepan was under Ma's bed. His heart almost stopped when he saw there wasn't two ten-pound notes any more. Just one plus a five pound note and a lot of coins. In something close to a fever, he counted it all out. Sixteen pounds and seventy-five pence! He shoved it all in his pocket with Grandpa's hankie on top to stop the clink of coins and went back to the kitchen. He was too strung up to finish his baked apple.

'I'll eat it for you,' Titch volunteered.

At last, everyone was finished.

He waited until they'd all gone to their rooms, fetched his rucksack, tied the arms of his jersey round his waist, the laces of his trainers on the strap of the rucksack and on bare feet and as quietly as he could, slipped out of the back door and on to the cliff path.

It was dusk but still light enough for him to find his way. There was something special about being out on his own at this time of night.

Almost as if the world was his alone and no one had discovered it before.

Soon he was going along the Creel Road where late night moths brushed against him, then silently past the lit windows of Seaview Terrace and down to the harbour. Down to *Nadzieja*. Down to *Hope*.

Dusk was turning to darkness. Oliver suddenly saw how Starwater got its name because at night all the stars seemed to fall into the sea.

He knew Cezary wouldn't come to the boat. They'd agreed it would only create suspicion. Even so, he couldn't help but wish that maybe Cheerio was there with his comforting wag-and-lick welcome.

A small ladder attached to the harbour wall let him climb down into the boat. Although there was no one around, he quickly ducked into the cabin. It was dark and smelt of fish and engine oil but it was cosy. There was one small bunk and Cezary had left two blankets.

Fear, guilt (about the borrowed money) and

excitement made him hungry. He ate two of his jam sandwiches, drank some water, checked that the money was safe, set the alarm clock for four forty-five. Through the portholes he could see moonlight on the water. Then as best he could, he snuggled down under the rough blankets. For what felt like hours he lay and listened to the fenders that hung from the hull bumping against the harbour wall and the boat creaking as it pulled against its moorings as if it too wanted to get away. Once he thought he heard the rotor blades of the helicopter that had buzzed around when he was with Cezary. Was that its searchlight flashing in the water? He was imagining things again. It was just the effect of moonlight. At last the slap of the sea and the boat's rhythmic rocking slowly made his eyes close. Moonlight washed over him.

He slept restlessly. In dream after dream he found Pa in dire trouble – tied up by bandits, trying to hop home on a broken leg, trapped under a falling roof – and in all these dreams (or nightmares) Oliver struggled to rescue him.

He didn't need the alarm clock. He woke to the sound of the bus coming down the hill into Starwater, its sudden shudder as it stopped, the slam of the driver's door, the murmur of voices.

Oliver grabbed his rucksack, combed his hair with his fingers, put on Pa's hat, said a silent thank you to Cezary and climbed out of the boat.

Bus number X254 was waiting.

CHAPTER 13

Bus Number X254

In the grey dawn, a small group of passengers was already huddled at the bus stop. As Oliver ran to join them, a woman with a heavy basket hurried down the hill and immediately began greeting everyone.

'Morning, Jack! Morning, Hilda! Promises to be a fine day. Morning, Stan!'

This last was to the driver who'd climbed out of the cab and was flexing his fingers as if preparing for a long drive. He was a skinny man with a thin thatch of once-blond hair and bright button eyes. He was wearing a checked shirt with the sleeves rolled up and a brown leather pouch fixed to his belt. It was for the fares,

Oliver realised, as the passengers began boarding, handing over their money. Stan wound out tickets from a clickedy old machine by the steering wheel. He seemed to know everyone by name and had a question for most of them.

How's your back today? Did the plumber come? Did you find your cousin? How's your lumbago?

It was like joining a club or a new family, Oliver thought, as he got his money ready. 'Going to Loch Wardle,' he said, trying to make his voice as confident as possible, as if he travelled on buses every day of the week.

'Oh aye, going all the way, are you?' said Stan. His bright eyes were kind but questioning. 'Pay half now, rest on the way back. Hope you've got your pieces, laddie! It's a long journey. Be late afternoon before we get there.'

'My pieces?' Oliver suddenly feared there was something very important he was missing.

'He means your sandwiches, love,' said the woman with the basket. She was sitting in front of him, sorting out the many items in her basket. 'For my daughter,' she explained. 'She's just had a third bairn. No time for cooking and shopping.'

Oliver smiled at her. He was wishing he'd brought more *pieces*. And why hadn't he worked out how long this journey would take?

The passengers were settling in. Coats were stowed up on the rack. Newspapers produced. Someone blew his nose loudly. A young woman, with a small suitcase pushed it under her seat, settled her hat in her lap and began talking to the man beside her.

'Everyone ready?' Stan called and there was a chorus of 'Yes!' and 'Let's go!' And, 'Put her in gear, Stan!' And they were off. Or almost off. It took Stan a few goes at the ignition for the engine to catch, a judder to go through the whole bus, a cheer from all the passengers and then they really *were* off.

It was a rattly old bus but no one seemed to mind. The bus rattled. The passengers chatted. About shopping, new babies, what so-and-so said to so-and-so.

The woman with the hat began a long story about a visit to her sister who lived far south in Whitstable. Half the bus seemed to be listening.

'That's Kent, you know,' she was saying. 'But it's right by the sea. My sister goes swimming every day, even when it's cold. She's got one of those wetsuits that keep you warm. She looks really funny in it but she doesn't care. Me, I can't swim. Somehow I never learnt when I was a girl. Soon as they took the waterwings off me, I sank. Anyway, I paddled and collected shells and my sister said . . .' Oliver thought of Titch and his shell collection and half wished he was with him.

As far as Oliver could tell there weren't any regular bus stops, or if there were, they didn't stop at them. New passengers just appeared at the roadside, waving Stan to a halt. Others, wanting to get off, simply tapped Stan on the shoulder, shouted 'Ta ta for now!' or 'See you later!' and then vanished down side roads or into woods or up a farm track. It was all so friendly that Oliver thought it was a bit sad when people got off. Might he see any of them 'later' or indeed ever again?

For an hour or so Stan drove along the coast. The bus would turn a corner or go down a hill and each time there would be a new view of the sea as if each one was a painter's attempt at making the sea bluer, more astonishing, more beautiful, wider and skyful.

After a while the bus turned inland. It wandered through woods where bluebells were beginning, trees turning all shades of green. It rattled happily through fields of early wheat and barley, sprinkled with poppies. There was a glimpse of farms and barns, sometimes a horse alone in a field, sometimes a huddle of sheep running away at the sound of the bus honking its horn round corners.

Oliver tried to remember the names of the villages they were passing through – Lanakmhor, Holmstir, Wantach – he wanted to be able to tell Cezary all about the journey. Once, as they were rounding a corner, a motorbike shot out and sped past them. Oliver thought he glimpsed a blue and green scarf before the driver disappeared down a side road. It probably meant nothing, he thought. Nobody, apart from Cezary, knew where he was going. He'd left a note in the kitchen that said *Don't worry. Back soon.* After all, this was quiet countryside. The rider probably lived locally. You were bound to see him every now and again. Even so, he shivered a little.

It was good to keep his eyes on Stan's hands, steady on the steering wheel.

The woman with the basket gave him an apple and a banana. The man behind him – Jack, was it? – offered him a marmite sandwich. Oliver relaxed. It was strange, but sitting on this bus with Stan at the wheel and these friendly passengers made him feel what was it? Well, as if he was at home! How could you be at home on a bus? Was home just somewhere you felt safe? With people you liked and who liked you?

Oliver was short of sleep. After a while, the

murmuring of voices merged with the bus's rattle and became a kind of lullaby. The woman with the hat continued her story. She and her sister went out for breakfast. 'Did you ever? Going out for breakfast? We went to a place called *Windy Corner*. No, it wasn't windy and we had . . .'

Without wanting to because he was enjoying the story, Oliver felt his eyes closing.

When he woke up the bus had stopped at the bottom of a steep hill and all the passengers had got off and were preparing to push. They seemed to enjoy it. Oliver got off and joined in. (In between puffs, the woman with the hat carried on with her story as she pushed. 'So I told her *puff* that I was thinking *puff puff* of getting married to Rowan *puff* and she said . . .') There was a lot of laughter with Stan revving the engine until it sounded quite painful and with a great effort the bus heaved itself up the hill.

'Does this happen often?' Oliver asked Jack, who looked too old to be pushing buses up hills and had gone red in the face.

'Every time,' was the answer. 'But Stan gets us there.'

Back on the bus, Oliver slept and woke and slept and woke. In between he ate most of his sandwiches, half his packet of biscuits, Jack's marmite sandwich and the apple and banana the woman with the basket had given him. He was desperate to know how much further it was to Loch Wardle, but didn't dare ask.

It was fresh and sunny now. The trees, looking newly green, made patterns of shadows on the road. A few of them were experimenting with May blossom. The early morning mist and dew had long cleared. A few clouds lingered as if they had nowhere to go. Morning slid into afternoon. Passengers came and went. Oliver lost all sense of time, he felt as if he'd been on Bus X254 for ever. This was how it was always going to be – a journey to find his pa that went on and on and on like an unending dream. It was mid-afternoon when he found himself the only passenger left.

CHAPTER 14

Stan

'Might as well move up near the front, laddie,' said Stan.

Oliver did as he was told. 'Where's everyone gone?' he asked.

'No one much lives up this way,' said Stan. 'There's a shepherd or two from Longnachty Farm and sometimes a mechanic comes up all the way from the city because something needs fixing. Doubt this service will keep going much longer. Nor this bus.' Stan patted his steering wheel sadly, much, Oliver thought, as if it were an old dog. The way Stan was with his bus made Oliver think of the way Grandpa was with his fiddle. Stan's shirt-sleeved arms were brown, his hands easy on the steering wheel. He was comfy with himself.

'Is it much further?' Oliver asked.

'Through the glen, two more lochs and we're there. Loch Wardle. End of my route. Where you off to, laddie?'

Oliver was relieved that there was no mention of Loch Ness or any monsters. His eyes met Stan's eyes in the driving mirror. Bright, questioning but kindly.

'I'm going to find my Pa,' he said. Oliver saw Stan's raised eyebrows.

'Going to find him, are you? Sounds as if you've lost him.'

'Well, not exactly,' said Oliver. 'Only he should have come home and he hasn't.'

'Umm,' said Stan. 'Maybe he doesn't want to be found?'

The suggestion sent a cold shiver down Oliver's back. In his dreams he'd heard Pa calling for help, dreamt of pulling him out from under a fallen roof, of giving him a piggy-back home but he'd never dreamt – and never, ever thought – of Pa not wanting to be found.

'Oh no,' he said loyally, though his hands had gone stone cold and there was a horrible feeling in his tummy, 'I'm sure he wants to be found. I've got a letter and a map and he says he loves us all. *Dearly*, that's what he says, *dearly*, even though . . .' Oliver hesitated, 'even though he says he hasn't always been a very good father.'

'Tell you what, laddie,' said Stan, 'my missus gave me some cake this morning and a nice bottle of lemonade. What say we have a little picnic together and talk this over?'

'Yes,' said Oliver. 'And I can show you the map.'

Stan parked the bus in a lay-by. The day had warmed up (as if it was having a rehearsal for summer) and so had the bus. Oliver had the notion that it was panting, much as a horse might.

'I'll leave the doors and windows open,' said Stan. 'Let her cool down.'

He produced two folding canvas stools,

a tub with two slices of cake (had his Missus known about him, Oliver wondered?) and a bottle of lemonade with two paper cups.

'Now then,' said Stan and a nice little breeze shivered the trees behind them cooling both them and the bus, 'tell me all about this pa of yours.'

So Oliver told him. First about *Dizzy Perch* and how it was far from anywhere, up in the clouds almost. How Pa had chosen *Dizzy Perch* to keep them safe. How they were home-schooled for the same reason (though neither Ma nor Grandpa always remembered). How *Dizzy Perch* was a sort of magical place but also lonely.

He told him about Ma and her books and Grandpa and his fiddle, about Lottie when she was Doctor Lott, about Titch collecting shells and pebbles and dancing in the middle of them. And somehow, as Stan listened and smiled, Oliver saw them all – Ma, Grandpa, Lottie and Titch – as Stan might see them, as jolly and a bit zany. And for the first time ever he felt glad to be a Coggin. It was as if being away from home, he could see them all, not just as Stan might see them, but properly, clearly. Why, his family were clever and talented and awkward and funny and sometimes lazy and often difficult but he loved them all dearly. Furthermore, he was very proud to belong to them.

'And your pa?' Stan prompted.

So Oliver told him about Pa's laboratory and how he was working on something very secret and important. A discovery perhaps. 'My pa has imaginative curiosity,' Oliver said.

'Does he now,' said Stan.

'Yes,' said Oliver, 'but he should have been home months ago and now we're running out of money and Ma's lovelorn ('Ah!' said Stan) and Titch isn't well and Grandpa's very old and, and, and . . .'

'And you're his firstborn son,' Stan finished. 'So this is your job.'

'I hadn't quite thought of it as a job,' said Oliver.

'Something about the oldest son,' said Stan,

'always has to take charge in the end. I was an oldest son myself. Took over this bus from my pa.'

Good lord, thought Oliver, was the bus that old? But Stan's words and his Missus's cake were making him feel better. Stronger. Ready to carry on. He took the map from his pocket. They spread it across their knees. Stan brushed away the cake crumbs.

'Auchterlaldy!' said Stan. 'Jings, your pa knows how to hide himself, that's for sure. It's a good few miles walk from Loch Wardle. I could take you a bit further on, but looking at this map, you've still got a fair walk – maybe even a bit of a climb ahead of you.'

Back on the bus the road seemed to narrow as if hardly anyone came this way. Now and again Stan had to pull the bus into a passing place to allow a car to zip past. Oliver counted the lochs. They lay still and mysterious, the water barely rippling, as if they held secrets in their depths that no one had yet disturbed.

'We're going through the Great Glen,' Stan

told him. 'It was made by glaciers millions of years ago. Watch out for waterfalls.'

Loch Wardle was the smallest one. 'Think of Goldilocks and the three bears,' said Stan. 'This is the baby loch.'

'No Goldilocks,' said Oliver. 'And no bears.'

'Not unless your pa has got a few teddies working for him!' said Stan.

Two miles further on, Stan brought the bus to its usual juddering halt.

'Wish I could take you further,' he said, 'but there isn't a road up to Auchterlaldy. Just that track you can see. Used to be a shepherd who had a cottage up there – he might still be around. If he is, tell him Stan says *hello.* You'd better take the rest of the lemonade with you. It's a thirsty walk up there. And listen, I'll be staying the night with my niece, Rhona, just near Loch Wardle. Place called Nixter. Talisker Cottage, Nixter. Got it? You could walk there if you had to. And remember, the bus'll be going back to Starwater tomorrow morning. I'll look out for you. And your pa. Good luck, laddie!'

Oliver stood at the bottom of the track and waved them away. But both Stan and the bus seemed reluctant to leave. After a while he heard the bus give three toots, each one fainter than the last.

Oliver looked up the track. It was shadowed by trees. Perhaps it was just the late afternoon sun, but a mist was slowly spreading from the top of the track down to where Oliver stood. It was a summery mist, a mix of rain and sunshine and there was a kind of magical stillness as if the air itself was holding its breath, waiting for something. Waiting for him?

A bird startled him as it flushed out of a tree and sped back through the Glen alarmed at being seen. A small train of ants ran past his feet. Standing there, feeling more alone than he'd ever felt in his life, Stan's question kept repeating itself over and over in his head – *maybe he doesn't want to be found? Maybe he doesn't want to be found?* As if in answer he distinctly heard a cuckoo calling *Sill-ee! Sill-ee! Sill-ee!*

At the bottom of the track there was a rough wooden signpost that said 'Auchterlaldy' in faded ink. There was no point in getting out the map. Unless Pa had moved somewhere else (an even more awful thought) he was obviously in the right place. But he got it out anyway, as a kind of talisman. After all, Pa himself had written on it. Marked the place with a red ring.

Well, he was oldest son, wasn't he? Oliver took a swig of Stan's lemonade as if taking a swig of courage and set off up the track.

CHAPTER 15

Pa

A few miles, that's what Stan had said about the track to Auchterlaldy. To Oliver they were the longest miles ever. It was two miles from *Dizzy Perch* to Starwater. This walk was twice as long. The track wound up and up until even the trees seemed to give up. It was as if spring had taken one look at the place and thought it wasn't worth bothering with. There was nothing but scrub, rough grass, stones, sky. He passed an almost derelict cottage, its stones gathering moss, its roof fallen in. If there ever had been an actual village of Auchterlaldy, there was no sign of it now. The whole place was bleak, abandoned.

Perhaps it was the mist, perhaps his nerves,

perhaps because he was looking up the track instead of down at his feet, but he'd only walked a mile or so when he stumbled and fell, gashing his leg on a stone he hadn't even noticed. It was a bad cut. Bad enough to make Oliver wonder if he might bleed to death and his corpse be found (if at all) by Pa or possibly crows. He sat down on a mossy tree stump and dug Grandpa's old hanky out of his rucksack. It was red and and large. He tied it round his leg as tightly as he could to stop the blood. At least it was the right colour.

It hurt a bit when he got up and set off on the track again. He could feel the hanky getting sodden. *I'm not going to look. I'm not going to look!* he told himself, for surely it couldn't be far now? Another mile. He must have done another mile. More. His leg was really aching now.

And then, just as he was running out of breath and thought he'd have to sit down and finish Stan's lemonade, he saw it. A long shack, a log cabin half hidden by a tumbledown stone wall. There was a thin wave of smoke coming out of the chimney and as he got nearer, and nearer, and nearer, his heart pounding, his mouth dry, he heard someone singing. Someone sounding happy. Someone singing a jolly song.

'When I was a lad I served a term
As office boy to an Attorney's firm.
I cleaned the windows and I swept the floor
And I polished up the handle of the big front
*   door.'*

Oliver forgot all about his leg. Something happened inside his head. It went off like an enormous PING! It exploded like a firework. It rushed the blood to his head. It made his hair stand on end. Oliver was so FURIOUS he thought he might burst.

Without a moment's thought, he dropped his rucksack on the ground, leapt the tumbledown wall without even looking to see if there was a gate, and although there wasn't a big front door and not even a handle on it, but just a latch (*so much for top secret*, he thought), he burst into . . . well, what had he burst into?

At the far end of the room there was a wood burning stove with a stack of logs beside it. There was a make-do bookshelf and a trestle table with the remains of lunch, a mug and a stack of magazines. There was a long bench fixed against the wall on which were ranged racks of test tubes. Coloured liquids glowed and bubbled inside them. Machines with dials and lights were plugged into the wall. Some possessed needles that wavered and trembled as if measuring something. Open on the bench was a large, leather-bound notebook with lots of incomprehensible scribbles on it – algebra, geometry, maybe words in Latin. This was it. This was the laboratory.

It was – the word took a minute to ping into Olly's head because it was so surprising – it was *homely*! This was Pa's home. This was where he was at home. And indeed there, in the middle of all these test tubes and mysterious machines, standing there with his mouth still open ready to finish his song, was Pa.

'Olly!' cried Pa and flung his arms wide in welcome.

'Pa!' shouted Oliver and hardly knowing what he was doing, rushed at him pummelling him with his fists, butting him with his head, kicking him with his feet all the time shouting, 'How could you? How dare you? Don't you know? Don't you know?' while the tears – and the tears seemed to be tears he'd been saving for years – ran down his cheeks and Pa tried in vain to stop the blows, saying, 'Olly! Olly, my dear, dear Olly!'

'I'm not! I'm not! I'm not your dear Olly!' Oliver shouted. For how *dare* he? How dare Pa stay away for months without a word and then call him *dear Olly*? Angry Olly was how he felt and he was about to say so. Then he fainted.

When he came round he was lying on a camp bed, pillows behind his head, a rug over his feet, a mug of tea beside him. No sign of Grandpa's bloody handkerchief. His leg had been washed clean. And when he sat up and looked at it there was no sign of the gash. The skin had knitted itself together as if it had never been cut. Oliver ran his hand down it. There must at least be a scar, he thought, but the skin was perfectly smooth.

Pa, comfy in a wicker chair, his feet up on a stool, was watching him and smiling.

'All better?' he asked.

'Well, yes!' said Oliver. 'How did that happen?'

Pa held up a tiny green tube. 'Coggin's Wound Healing Tincture,' he said. 'Works easily on the outside of the body. But I've been experimenting so that it could be used internally. During operations, for instance. Just might save a few lives.'

'That's your discovery?' asked Oliver.

'Well, yes,' said Pa. 'And whether you like it or not, you are my dear, dear Olly.'

Oliver grunted and rubbed his eyes. His face was still tear-stained.

'You forgot us,' he said. He was trying to do in his head what felt like an important sum.

Was discovering something that would heal wounds inside and outside of a person's body, that might save a few lives, more important than remembering to be home when your family expected you? Needed you? More important than being a father? What was it he'd heard Grandpa say? *In my opinion being a father is more important than being a discoverer.* Oliver looked at his leg and thought the question was impossible to answer.

'You look so . . .' Oliver hesitated because there was another lump in his throat, 'so at home here. When . . . when you should be at home with *us*!'

Pa shifted his shoulders up and down. 'Well, maybe a person has several homes,' he said. 'A home for the heart. A home for the head. A country that's home. A home with people you love.'

Oliver thought of Cezary coming from another country to live in Starwater. 'At home in the world,' he said.

'That too,' said Pa.

Oliver sat up straight in the camp bed. There

was a lot to think about. It was all very well for Pa to heal the gash on his leg. That was, well, awesome. But there was something like a gash, a cut, a hurt in Oliver's heart and that wasn't better yet.

'Have you any idea what month this is?' he asked.

Pa looked out of the window. 'Well, I suppose it is quite warm,' he said guiltily, 'so maybe it's a bit later than February.'

'It's almost *June*,' said Oliver. He found himself still feeling angry. All those days, weeks and months of worry! The nights he couldn't sleep! How very difficult it had been finding out where Pa was. The loneliness. Most of all the *missing*. But what could you do when your ma or pa didn't do what a ma or pa should? A parent could punish a child. But could a child punish a parent? Not that Oliver even thought of that. His anger was mixed with relief. Relief and – well – triumph! He'd made it, hadn't he? Made it on his own. Here he was up in the Highlands in a log cabin laboratory. And with his pa.

'There are scientists all over the world

wanting this stuff,' said Pa. 'You see, in the wrong hands, used in reverse so to speak, it could be used like a virus to *make* wounds just by adding the smallest amount of a certain chemical. I've had to concentrate awfully hard. That's why I'm late. I've only just finished. Only just got it right.'

Oliver considered. Pa waited. A telling off, Oliver thought. That's what Pa deserves, a Very Serious Telling Off before I mention how very, very, VERY pleased I am to have found him.

'Grandpa's very old,' said Oliver.

'I know, I know!' said Pa.

'He doesn't want to die before you come home.'

'I know, I know. I promised him . . .' said Pa.

'Titch is poorly,' said Oliver.

Pa put his head in his hands.

'We've almost run out of money,' said Oliver.

Pa clapped his hand to his forehead. 'How could I forget?' he asked.

'That's what I've been wondering,' said Oliver. 'And Ma's lovelorn,' he finished.

'Olly, my dear, my dear, dear Olly. Thank you for coming. I think it's time we went home.' Pa looked about him. For a moment he looked sad. Then he clapped his hands together as if he'd made a decision. 'Come on, Olly,' he said. 'We've got to shut this place down.'

It took the two of them the rest of the afternoon. The machines were switched off after Pa had examined the dials and made more notes. The contents of the test-tubes were poured into jars and put into a lead-lined storage box. The leather-bound notebook was packed into a large bag. A jumble of Pa's clothes were stuffed on top.

Pa made them both scrambled eggs on his cooking ring and buttered lots of bread to go with them. They ate sitting on stools at the trestle table. Oliver thought it was the best meal he'd ever eaten. It was growing dark, but inside the log cabin laboratory it was warm and cosy.

Oliver thought of *Dizzy Perch*, and how it was at night, strange and magical up in the clouds. Ma, Grandpa, Titch, Lottie, they'd surely be missing him by now. Perhaps loving and missing were two feelings that often went together. You wouldn't miss someone unless you loved them.

'Stan's bus,' he said, 'goes tomorrow morning from Loch Wardle.'

'Oh,' said Pa, 'I don't think we need to wait for that.'

Oliver wondered if Pa intended them to walk all the way back to *Dizzy Perch*. Would they walk through the night? Another word pinged into his head. *Eccentric*. That's what his Pa was.

Right now, Pa was shutting down the woodburning stove by chucking sand on it from a bucket kept beside it. He was turning off first the lights, then the humming generator that had given him electricity. He was locking and bolting the front door. Putting books away. Looking about him.

'Hurry up, Olly,' he said.

'Hurry up!' said Oliver. 'Have you got magic

roller skates or something? Are you hoping to thumb a lift? Nothing can get up this track!'

'Out the back,' said Pa.'

'What? Where? Why?' Oliver stammered, but he followed as Pa, with a last look behind him, led the way out through a small door at the back. He locked and bolted it. Slipped on a padlock.

In the dusk Oliver could see nothing but a flat, stony plateau. Then he saw it. Something yellow whirling down out of the sky. And there it was like a large yellow bird, the helicopter he'd seen in the sky above Starwater. And out of it, scrambling out of the pilot's door, jumping down, taking off his headphones, a man wearing a blue and green scarf.

'Meet Joe,' said Pa, 'my old pal Joe. He's been keeping an eye on you, Olly.'

Joe took off his pilot gloves and stretched out his hand to Oliver.

'Hi, Oliver,' he said. 'Pleased to meet you properly at last. Almost feel I know you, I've been watching you for so long. You've not been easy to follow, I can tell you that!'

The two shook hands. 'I saw you at the bus stop,' said Oliver. 'Then I saw you on a motorbike. And one day I thought I saw you on the beach and Ma was waving to you. And when I was in Starwater I kept seeing or hearing the helicopter. You kept turning up in so many different ways I began to think I was hallucinating!

Joe laughed. 'I needed both the motorbike and the helicopter,' he said. 'And you nearly caught me out when Ma waved at me. I've known your Ma almost as long as I've known your Pa. Your Pa's my oldest friend. He's helped me in the past. My turn to help him. Let's not be strangers any more. Friends?'

'Friends!' said Oliver. They shared a quick, shy hug.

All three were about to climb into the helicopter when Oliver said, 'Stan! I've got to say goodbye to Stan.'

'Where is he?' asked Joe.

'He's staying with his niece, Rhona. Talisker

Cottage, Nixter. That's what he said.'

'I can fly low,' said Joe. 'I'll hover over it. The noise will bring him out.'

They lifted off, Oliver sitting close to his Pa in the window. Joe kept the helicopter just above the level of the trees until they came to a clearing with a small cottage. There was a light in the window. Stan's bus was parked at the side. Joe dropped a little lower and they hovered over the cottage making the trees blow in sudden alarm.

Out first came Rhona, worriedly scanning the sky, shading her eyes with her hand. Then came Stan, hands on hips, about to shake his fist at them. Joe slid open the helicopter window. Oliver pushed his head out as far as he could.

'Stan! Stan!' he shouted. 'I've found him! I've found my Pa! We're going home to *Dizzy Perch*!'

They couldn't hear Stan's reply. They just saw him grin and give Oliver a big thumbs-up.

About the author

Diana Hendry grew up by the sea and now lives in Edinburgh. She has published more than forty books for children and teenagers, including *Harvey Angell*, which won the Whitbread (now Costa) Award in 1991 and has been translated into many languages and is still in print. More recently, her young adult novel *The Seeing*, was shortlisted for the Costa Award. As a poet, Diana has published six collections of poetry for adults and two for children plus a libretto for a musical version of *The Pied Piper of Hamelin*.

Diana began her writing career as a reporter and feature writer on provincial newspapers. She frequently tutors courses in creating writing – including the teenage winners of the Pushkin Prizes in Scotland. She has given poetry readings, workshops and talks to children and adults at numerous festivals and schools throughout the UK.

For a year, Diana was writer-in-residence at Dumfries and Galloway Royal Infirmary and later became a Royal Literary Fund Fellow at Edinburgh University. Currently, she is co-editor of *New Writing Scotland*.

More about Diana on her website: www.dianahendry.co.uk